Darkness Fades

Jessica Sorensen

Jessica Sorensen

Darkness Fades

For information:

http://jessicasorensensblog.blogspot.com/

Cover Design and Photo by Mae I Design and Photography

www.maeidesign.com

Darkness Fades—Book 3

ISBN : 978-1492979340

Jessica Sorensen

Chapter 1

I feel like I'm dying. Over and over again. Maybe that is what I'm doing. Being beaten to the point where I will die so I can heal and start the process all over again. Over and over and over.

Life then death. Life then death. Life.

I've been staring at the same ceiling for so long that I've memorized every small crack and divot. The smell of the air is forever branded in my nostrils and what happened here will linger in my heart. The day Gabrielle captured me and Monarch stepped out as a higher; the man who I once thought of a father gone. I've been beaten repeatedly since by Gabrielle and his Watchers, who work for the Highers and guard The Colony I used to live in, like they're testing me for weaknesses. I've actually learned a few things about the Watchers since I've been here. 1) Is that they're almost as disgusting as the vampires underneath the masks, something that I discovered during a fight I had with one of them and I managed to rip off their mask. They have no skin. At all. Which makes them sensitive to light and air and any sort of touch, which is probably why they wear the mask.

And 2) Monarch helped create them. But I wasn't surprised by that, since he helped create almost everything except for humans.

Every bone in my body throbs as my muscles battle to heal. The silver the Highers injected through my veins has slowed my healing process, making the injuries and wounds harder to bare. I can take it, though. I can take much more, if I have to.

I lift my head off the cold, concrete floor and examine my wounds. My arms are dotted with blues and purples; bruised and scratched. There's dried blood in my long, black hair and it also coats my clothes. My face is covered with gashes and at the same time it feels like my nose and jaw are either broken or dislocated.

I want to keep fighting, yet it's becoming harder to endure the pain. I'm exhausted, beaten to the core, no energy left in me. Finally, I let myself fall back down to the floor and my eyes drift shut.

"Tell me why Aiden's going to die," I demand to Monarch as I stand in a small room with concrete walls.

Monarch stands near the doorway in his white coat, his voice trembling as he answers, "Because I messed up when I created him. I really did. And unless he changes his mind about his existence, he won't survive... I'm so sorry."

"When does he die?" My voice sounds surprisingly choked. I ball my hands into fists and step forward. "Tell me," I demand.

He swallows hard, shifting his weight. "Soon, unless you can change his mind about life and death."

Blinding pain radiates in my jaw and nose, and my eyes fly open. I sit up, slapping my hands over my mouth as the bones in my face realign themselves into position, the muscles and tissues around them healing. The pain is blindingly intense, more than any other pain I've felt during my existence. I almost want to scream bloody murder, but I won't give Gabrielle or anyone else the satisfaction.

After what seems like forever, the pain subsides and I remove my hand, letting out a breath of relief. I trace my fingers along my newly healed legs and arms, my cheeks, jaw and my nose. I'm as good as new. Not even a scratch.

I'm about to relax back, try to rest before it starts all over again, but then the lights suddenly flash off. Darkness suffocates me, surrounds me, traps me even more than I already am. Yet I can sense someone is nearby, watching me.

I push to my feet and walk over to the glass wall of my cell. I press my hand to the glass then stare into the darkness, searching for whoever's out there. My night vision is an excellent asset and I can see a lot, including the glass cages around me. Each one appears empty, but I know they're not.

"Gabrielle," I call out. "I know you're out there."

He doesn't respond and I'm not surprised. He enjoys messing with my head. Thrives off it. He's been chasing after me since he discovered that I have strength that only the Highers are supposed to have and now that I've become a Day Taker, he only wants to torture me more.

I turn around to sit back down on the floor, the darkness blinding me, and cold fingers wind around my neck, choking the oxygen right of my lungs. I open my mouth to scream, but the fingers delve deeper into my skin, pushing against my throat so forcefully that I know that the bones are on the verge of breaking.

Then a hand winds tightly around my arm and I'm pulled back. The fingers leave my throat to be replaced roughly over my mouth. I throw my head back against the face of my attacker, but they dodge to the side. I miss. I jab my elbow backward, grazing their rock solid chest. The stranger hops back, still holding onto me, their hand then clamps down on my mouth tighter. I raise my foot to kick them in the shin, but they maneuver us around in a small circle, throwing me off balance, and I almost fall to the floor.

Infuriation and frustration cause me to bring my fangs out. The pointed teeth slip sharply from my gum lines, unhinging my jaw before they snap, digging into the hand.

The person tenses, but quickly relaxes. "Shh…" a familiar voice whispers in my ear.

"Aiden?" With one swift throw of my weight, I shove him off and spin around. His arms fall from me and I tuck my fangs back into my mouth. "What are you doing here?"

He squints at me through the darkness then dares a step towards me, brushing his dark hair out of his eyes. He studies me momentarily with caution then grabs my hands and cups them in his, his skin notably warm.

"Tristan came back," he says. "He told us the Highers came after you..." His eyes sweep me over as if he's checking for wounds. "That they had Watchers with them and that you and Sylas were captured then taken prisoner."

I nod warily. "Yeah, but how did you get in here?" I turn around to look at the cage door behind me, noticing it's open. I also notice that it's really quiet. Deadly quiet.

Where are the guards?

I turn back to Aiden and cross my arms, stepping back, putting a little distance between us because I'm not sure if I trust him. He's not the strongest person and the fact that he got inside here... it doesn't make any sense. "Weren't there Watchers guarding the cages?"

He nods, his honey eyes relentlessly locked on me as a cocky smile spreads across his face. "Yeah, there were quite a few Watchers, but I convinced them that they should go take a break."

I take another step back as more suspicion arises. "That doesn't even sound possible... they wouldn't simply go take a break because you told them to?"

"You don't think so?" he questions with a cock of his eyebrow. "Actually, I can be really persuasive when I try."

Something's wrong. This isn't right. This isn't the Aiden I know. Something's different about him. But what? I assess him through the dark and notice that he does look a little bit different. His eyes are a hue darker and almost matching his hair. His skin looks paler, but in a strange, healthy way. It has a bluish tint to it, as though his veins have become more defined.

"Oh my God." It hits me, like a kick to the gut, and the wind gets slammed out of me. "Why did you... how did you...? You're a Day Taker now?"

His smile is my only answer.

Chapter 2

"Why?" I whisper, inching farther away from him. It's not like I'm worried that I won't be able to handle myself if I need to fight him. I'm just not sure what the Day Taker version of Aiden is going to be like. He could be a lot different from the guy I first met—maybe even dangerous.

"You told me you didn't want to be one. That being a Day Taker was the wrong choice—that being human was right and now..." I pause at the lack of life in his eyes. *It's real. He's really one of them. Why am I reacting so strangely over this?* "Why did you do it?"

"That's not important right now." His fingers enfold around my arm and then he jerks me towards the open door. "We need to get out of here before the guards or one of the Highers comes out and finds us." He then releases my arm and shoves at my back, pushing me out the door.

I slam to halt in the hallway just outside the cell. "I'm not going anywhere until I find Sylas. When we got separated... and... something happened to him, Aiden. He's been infected by something and he... he needs our help."

Aiden shakes his head. "No way. We have to go."

I shake my head and stand firm, ready to fight. "I refuse to go without him."

He rakes his fingers roughly through his hair, glancing behind him and then behind me. "We're running out of time, Kayla. We need to go. Now."

Deep down, I know he's probably right. The logical thing would be to get the hell out of here before Gabrielle shows up, or a Watcher, but I stand firm, keeping my boots planted to the floor, refusing to budge. "I'm. Not. Going. Without. Him."

I can't leave Sylas here, especially if he's changing into some kind of mutated, hybrid beast. I need to find him and see if he is still... well, Sylas. If he's not... I'll keep my promise and end his life. No matter how difficult it is. I'm tough. Strong. Plus, letting him become a beast is worse than death.

Aiden rakes his fingers through his hair again and then lets out a frustrated sigh. "All right, hurry up and search the other cages, but if he's not in them, we have to go... we'll come back and look for him later, when things cool off."

He's lying. I can feel it flowing off him, vile and foul. However, it doesn't really matter. He may want to pretend like he's in charge, but when it all comes down to it, I'm not leaving without Sylas. I'll even kick his ass if I have to.

I nod, pretending I'm agreeing, and then run down the hall lined with cells, relishing in my freedom, which will only taste better when Sylas has freedom, too. God knows what they've done to him, if he's still alive, or what he even looks like. Is there even a Sylas left to save? Sylas was once a Day Taker, which is a thing between a vampire and a human. But I haven't seen him since he revealed that he'd been bitten by what I call an abomination; a disgusting creature that makes vampires look good. They're strong though, big, and foul, and like to feed off the flesh and blood of humans. And Sylas could be one of them… and probably is and that thought hurts my heart in a way that I'm not used to.

I check in each cell as I pass by. There's fresh blood on the floors and it splatters across the walls, but each cell is empty. As I reach the final cell, my quiet, dead heart drops in my chest because Sylas isn't there.

"Kayla, come on," Aiden says. "We have to go."

"No, I'm not going." I jerk my arm away from him as he grabs a hold of it. "I'm not giving up yet."

"Juniper." His voice is sharp as he jerks on my arm. "I'm not going to let you stay here longer."

It takes all my energy not to knock him to the floor. I dig my feet into the ground, ready to kick his ass; my fist clenching, my muscles winding into knots. Then I hear the soft thud of approaching footsteps and my anger turns to tension. As my head snaps in the direction the noise is coming from, I spot the dark outline of a tall figure moving in our direction.

"If you don't go," Aiden tries one more time as he tugs on my arm, "then hope for humanity is lost. You're the one who has to save everyone, Kayla. Now please, come on. We'll come back for Sylas. I promise." This time I don't feel a lie flowing off him.

I hesitate as the figure moves closer. I know he's right, yet I'm so conflicted it feels as though my body is being ripped in half. I want to stay, yet I need to go. Go. Stay. Go. Spinning around in the opposite direction, I grab Aiden by the hand. "Come on, let's go." It hurts to say it, and I feel like I'm going to throw up with each stride I take, yet I fight it, moving forward.

Holding onto my hand, he leads me to the right and we run as the footsteps chase after us. The lights above our heads flicker on and off, shadows dancing along the walls as we race towards the hole in the wall that was once the red door. As we're about to reach it, an eruption of shouts echo from behind us.

I risk a quick glance over my shoulder while I keep moving forward. Gabrielle stands by the entrance of the cell that I was locked in only minutes before. He takes in the sight of the empty room then his gaze jerks in our direction.

"Go get them!" he yells, the anger in his voice reverberating down the hallway.

The Watchers stay frozen in place, filling up the hallway, with masks covering their faces. They refuse to move and finally, Gabrielle shoves one of them in our direction.

"Get moving," he shouts, however the Watcher simply trips, regains his balance and then stands motionless, watching Aiden and I run without chasing us.

Gabrielle's pale eyes burn with rage as he reaches over and snatches hold of one of the Watcher's arms, jerking them close to him. His fangs descend and then he plunges the tips of them into the Watcher, who grows limp as Gabrielle drinks from his body, slurping the blood like it's a drink until finally he releases the Watcher and the body slumps to the floor. A look of satisfaction arises on Gabrielle's face as he stares down at the dead Watcher. Then he reaches up and wipes the blood off his face with the back of his hand before he raises his eyes back up to me. Our gazes lock and a silent exchange takes place; he'll come after me. I know it, feel it, see it.

Suddenly, a blur of white moves up behind Gabrielle and his head snaps in the direction of the object. I stumble over my feet as I struggle to see what it is, but it's too blurry, too dark. Wait a minute... Monarch.

He steps out from behind Gabrielle at the same time his eyes lock on Aiden and I as we bend down to dive through the hole in the wall. As he disappears out of my sight, a slightly satisfied grin rises on his face.

"Kayla, come on!" Aiden's voice jerks me back to reality as he tugs my arm, hauling me the rest of the way through the hole.

We scramble all the way through and dive headfirst into a dark room, landing on our knees. Aiden quickly pulls me to my feet. I blink several times as my eyes gradually adjust to the inadequate light.

"How do we get out of here?" I ask Aiden, glancing at the four walls, floor and ceiling. The only noticeable way out is the hole we just dove through.

"Just a second." Aiden scans the darkness, tensing when the vampires cry out from just outside of the walls; hungry and ready to feed or infect. Just like that hybrid beast did with Sylas. God, I feel icky… guilty maybe…

Aiden walks over to the corner of the room with his hand out in front of him until his fingers brush a piece of plastic. He lifts it up and on the other side of it is a vacant road.

"What the hell?" I mutter, hurrying over to him.

He sticks his head out after taking a cautious glance outside. Then he steps out, holding up the piece of plastic, motioning for me to follow.

I hesitate, glancing over my shoulder, torn on what do to. "Where are we going?"

"To the only place we have left to go," he says and I look back at him. "Back to the cave where I left everyone."

I dither a few seconds longer, struggling with my morals, and then irrevocably step out into the street. The sky is dark; covered with grey clouds and smoke. Debris litters the ground and fires burn in the distance, reminding me that there are still problems and dangers to face.

Aiden and I begin to run towards the park where we used to play when we were kids. The ground is a sheet of ash and the remaining trees are charred. Vampire cries echo all around us, but I can't seem to spot a damn one. It seems like we're running for hours and, although I don't grow tired, I start to get impatient.

Aiden is the complete opposite; he seems content as he easily runs while taking even strides. He's also seems more confident and less afraid of the world. It makes me question if he's glad he chose not to stay human, even after all his negativity directed towards the choice. Maybe now that he's tasted what it's like, he's glad he did it and regrets that he didn't do it sooner. Or maybe it merely changed him enough that he lost who he was before he became a Day Taker.

We finally slow down when it feels like we're a safe distance away from the cells and are just outside of the city limits where abandoned buildings stretch toward the smoky sky. I turn and look at the building where I was a held as a prisoner; it looks like a little dot now in the distance. My eyes scan the terrain around us and I allow myself to relax when I don't see any movement. We're not being followed. Good. But why?

I look back towards Aiden who is staring at me quietly in the dark. I remember that he still hasn't answered my question, what the hell happened to make him decide to become one of us?

"What?" he turns away from me and his eyes lock on the terrain where fires crackle and smoke rises in the night sky. "Why are you staring at me?"

"Because you never answered my question," I say, crossing my arms. "Why did you change?"

He's silent for forever, either avoiding my question or considering it; it's hard to tell because I find his new demeanor hard to read. Finally, he sighs. "Do you really not know the answer to that already?" He slants his head to the side and our gazes meet. His expression is intense. His eyes are burning with passion. It kind of throws me off a little, enough that I take a step back. "It was for you, Juniper."

"That doesn't make any sense. You hated that I chose to become a Day Taker myself. You even told me that I wasn't me anymore—that I wasn't even human," I remind him. "Why would you want to throw all your beliefs away because of me?"

"Because of Maci." Maci is the little girl who was thrown out of The Colony with me during The Gathering and she just happens to be able to see the future, although she never gives anyone specific details just hints, which can get frustrating.

He hesitates then moves to the side, getting close to me, and then he reaches for my hand, lacing our fingers together. Despite my initial reaction to jerk my hand back, I just stand there and let him hold it, confused.

"When Tristan told us that you were captured, Maci said you were going to die, and so would the world. I told you earlier that I'd always be there for you. And I meant it. Whatever it takes, I'll be there for you; even if it means turning into my own worst enemy."

I can sense that he wants to kiss me, and before I can do anything about it, he pulls me into him. As he leans in, I battle with my confliction. Part of me wants to kiss him, for reasons I can't even process at the moment; however, the other part of me knows it's wrong. I'm about to lean away, listening to my final thought, when the other side of me pushes through.

I want to kiss him. I want him more than anything else in the world. I want him more than Sylas. We belong together.

I blink, wondering where the thought came from.

Aiden reaches down and fixes a finger under my chin. He gently tilts my head up towards his with his fingertips, his eyes shutting as his lips inch towards mine. He's breathing raggedly, his chest colliding with mine. If I had a heartbeat, I'd bet it'd be racing.

My eyes remain open as I cup the back of Aiden's neck, about to kiss him, but then I picture Sylas. His eyes, his cocky attitude that makes him annoying, yet at the same time, I can't seem to stay away from him. Deep down, I know I want to be kissing him. *What am I doing? What am I thinking? Why am I ready to kiss Aiden?*

No, I want to kiss Aiden.

No Sylas.

Aiden.

Shit. I'm so confused.

It clicks what's going on. Shaking my head, I remove my hand from Aiden's neck and push him away. He jumps back, startled, and then stumbles ungracefully over his feet a little, clutching onto my hand for support. His eyelids lift open and confusion masks his expression. "What's wrong Juniper?"

"Why did you just do that?" I ask, slipping my hand from his hold.

"What? Try to kiss you?" he asks, gaping at me like I've lost my mind. "Because I wanted to."

"Well, don't do that," I tell him, swallowing hard.

"Why not?"

"Because I don't want you to. And stay out of my head."

Shaking his head, he turns his back to me. "It would have been a great kiss if you wouldn't have lost your damn mind and shoved me away." He starts to stalk away, but I jump in front of him.

"Lost my mind? You were in my mind... you were manipulating my thoughts." I push him, but this time he doesn't stumble. "I could feel you inside my head. You were making me feel those things... like I *wanted* to kiss you—*wanted* to be with you."

I shove him again, this time much harder, and the force launches him in the air much harder than I intended. I fold my arms across my chest and cringe as he crashes into a vehicle just behind us. Metal bends and concaves under his weight then ashes scatter and float in the air.

Aiden lands on the ground hard, asphalt debris shattering under his weight. He quickly gets to his feet, and with three long strides, he closes the distance between us. He leans into my face, anger burning in his eyes as he balls his fists. For a second, I think he is going to attack me, but I just stare at him, refusing to back away. When he raises his fist, making me think he's going to hit me, I turn to leave, not wanting to fight. Not right now. Not here. Not when there are other things I need to take care of.

He captures me by the elbow as I start to storm away, stopping me in my tracks. I turn my head and try to shrug him off. "Let go of me."

Aiden's eyes widen in shock. "Juniper, I'm not going to hurt you."

I shake my head in disbelief as I glance at his hand on my arm, his fingertips digging into my skin. "You're not?" I question with doubt.

He releases my arm and then rakes his fingers through his hair. "I would never hurt you. You have to believe that I wouldn't."

I sigh because I can actually feel that he's telling the truth. "I believe…" I trail off, my eyes wandering to my left at something heading towards us… something large.

Aiden follows my gaze and his eyes snap wide as the creature weaves in a fast pattern between the cars in the road. We take off at the same time, sprinting in the opposite direction as fast as our legs will carry us. Yet, I can hear the panting of the creature getting closer the ground cracking beneath its feet as it runs on all fours.

When I glance over my shoulder, I realize just how big of a problem we have. There's not just one, there are many creatures chasing after us in a herd. Their fleshless bodies are a repulsive sight to behold, their fangs out, nipping as saliva drips from their mouths. My conscious starts to nag me with guilt because they're the same creatures that bit Sylas. Or as Dominic called them, vampire abominations. It reminds me that Sylas could very easily be one of them.

Chapter 3

I speed up, my arms pumping, my feet moving so fast that they're nearly gliding across the ground. Aiden stays right behind me, whether on purpose or not, I'm not sure.

The mutilated monsters howl and nip at our heels; the sound forces my legs to move quicker than I ever thought was possible. I nearly fly as I race towards a wide trench in the distance. Approaching it, I glance over my shoulder as I leap into the air, relieved to see Aiden is right behind me, flying over the trench as if it's the easiest thing to do in the world. I'm glad he can keep up. Although I hate to admit it, it drove me a little bit crazy when he was human and slowed me down.

When my feet gracefully land on the ground, I hurry to my left and head for the desert land that stretches towards the caves. Aiden gets his footing and moves quickly with me, motioning at me to go faster. So I do. My legs and arms drive my body past its breaking point until I feel like I'm going to crack apart. But even then, I go faster.

The monsters begin to fade into the distance, however their howls and cries still pierce the air, so I keep moving; going forward, racing through the sand, around bushes, cacti, my eyes fixed ahead of me. I could probably go on for days, but I eventually slow my pace down to a jog then conclusively to a walk when I feel we're safe enough away and the howls have finally dissipated.

Aiden slows down with me, walking at my side while looking content and sort of happy, which is strange.

He's not panting, nor am I. Our hearts aren't beating, but our skin is damp with sweat. We're both unnaturally calm and it starts to click in my head that maybe we're abominations, too.

"So are you going to tell me what those things are?" Aiden finally asks, peering up at the dark sky.

"I'm not one-hundred percent sure." I shrug as I side-step around a bush. "All I know is that's what Dominic turned into—and he said he was an abomination. Half vampire, half human... some sort of mutated hybrid."

Aiden slams to a stop. "Wait, isn't that what we are? A mutated hybrid?"

I halt and turn to face him. "Well, Dominic said we weren't. He said we're something different, although he never said exactly what, but the abominations are more vampire than human. They are gross beasts with no sense of pain, fear or mercy that will kill anything. *We* still have our will left—our sense of humanity—for the most part." I breathe in quietly and gaze out at the land. "I probably could have learned more about them, but I ended up killing Dominic when he attacked... Sylas and me."

"Have you ever seen them in groups before?" he asks, leaning to the side and catching my eye, his expression un-emotional. "The beasts, I mean?"

I shake my head. "I've only seen two and they were by themselves."

"Where did they come from?" he wonders. "I mean, I've never seen one before, so why so many all of a sud-den? And why were they running in packs like that?"

"I'm not sure... maybe Monarch and Gabrielle are cre-ating them now. That would explain the sudden onset of them."

"Why would you think that?"

"Because of the cells. There was blood and scratches all over inside them... and I heard stuff... horrible stuff..." I trail off, trying not to shudder because it'd make me look weak. "I think that they may have been creating them there and that they might be using them as weapons, sending them out to attack on command."

Since I'm divulging everything right now, I decide to let him in on everything, unsure how he'll react. "Aiden, there's something I need to tell you about Sylas... when he was attacked by Dominic... he was... he was bit. He started changing into..." I shut my eyes and force a lump down my throat. "Something else when we were captured by the Highers. I'm not sure *what* he is right now." When I finish, I open my eyes.

"So you're saying he's going to turn into one of those monsters?" he asks, his voice tight.

"You sound upset."

"Because I am," he replies, his jaw set tightly.

"But I thought you hated him."

"I don't hate him." He looks at me and I see honesty burning in his eyes. "Just because he's done some things in the past that I think are wrong, it doesn't mean that I don't care about him. Besides, I wouldn't want anyone to have to become one of those things." He starts walking again and I follow him.

I allow my thoughts drift to Sylas as silence settles between Aiden and I. I can't help thinking of the kiss Sylas and I shared before we were captured in the cells. The way his lips felt against mine, the strange emotions I had, how much I liked it, how much I want to do it again, *feel* all those things again. Anger swells inside me. Sylas shouldn't have to suffer.

You don't want to kiss him again... you just think you do. I kick a rock in my path and it flies up in the air, almost hitting Aiden in the back.

Wait a minute, Aiden.

Rushing up behind him, I quickly snatch hold of the back of his shirt and jerk him to a stop. Then, I tug him around to face me. "You never told me what the hell was going on back there." I point over my shoulder. "When you were trying to kiss me... it felt like you were putting thoughts into my head, like you were trying to manipulate my thoughts."

He smiles at me arrogantly and I have to resist the urge to slap him. "I was just trying to help you. Deep down inside, you really want to be with me and so I was giving you a little push."

I shake my head and shove him out of my way, stepping around him and heading for the cave that's in the rocky cliff not too far from here. "I'm warning you now, never to do that again or you'll pay," I threaten, however I'm not sure if I really mean it.

"I'm sorry," he says, but I can hear the smile in his voice. "It worked so well on the guards that I wanted to test it on you. I'd never force you to do anything and I would have stopped it if I thought you didn't really want to." He catches up with me and captures my gaze. "Do you forgive me?"

I shrug because I'm not sure if I do or not.

The cave rests in an area that is surrounded by cliffs. The sun is almost rising by the time we reach the entrance, which is blocked by a boulder to keep out the vampires.

After we breezily climb up the side of the hill, I slide the boulder out of the way then duck down and step inside, Aiden following right behind me. He doesn't bother closing the entrance back up, since the sun will be up soon and the abominations and vampires only come out at night.

Everyone is fast asleep in the back section of the cave, but the noise we make ends up waking everyone. Maci opens her eyes and immediately jumps up, squealing as she runs towards me and wraps her arms around me. I awkwardly return her enthusiastic hug, giving her a pat on the back.

Her eyes sparkle with excitement as she pulls away. "Kayla, I knew you'd make it back alive, just like I knew Aiden would save you. I really missed you."

"I missed you, too." I pat her on the head then pry her arms away from me, so she skips off to hug Aiden.

I sit down on the dirt floor, lean my back against the rock walls and shut my eyes, feeling Tristan's eyes on me from the corner of the cave.

"Where's Sylas?" he asks.

I open my eyes and look at him for a moment, wondering if I seem as different as he does. "He—"

Maci cuts me off, moving in front of me. "Sylas is gone," she announces sadly.

Greyson steps out from a dark corner of the cave, his hands tucked in the pockets of his pants. His red hair is sticking up all over the place and his brows are furrowed. "You mean he is dead?" he asks Maci.

"No, not dead, just gone," she says and then whispers, "He's something different now."

Everyone looks at me, but all I can do is stare at Maci. *Gone. Sylas is gone. I feel like I can't breathe.*

32

"What do you mean he's something different?" I ask Maci, getting to my feet.

"I mean he's not a Day Taker," she says simply.

Aiden says something to me, but I can't seem to find my voice. He's not a Day Taker anymore, which means what? I think I know, but it hurts to admit it.

Sylas has become an abomination.

Chapter 4

Is he really one of those hideous monsters? Will he be sent to kill us? My thoughts make me sick and the sensation only heightens when everyone simply stares at me, as if they're waiting for me to explain. But I can't—won't. I refuse to accept it yet. I can't breathe.

I swiftly get to my feet and head to the entrance, walking into the daylight. I stop on the side of the hill, breathing in the cool breeze, trying to erase the feelings inside me, yet they remain.

Aiden walks towards me, but pauses at the entrance where the shade and the light meet. Now that he has changed into a Day Taker, he can't step out into the sunlight. He's pretty much trapped inside that cave until sundown.

"Kayla, please relax," he begs.

I don't turn around. "Aiden, please leave me alone… I just need a small break for a moment," I tell him and then hike further down the hill. I'm not sure where I'm going, only that I need to move; clear my head for a moment.

I work my way to the side of the cliff until I find a spot where I climb to the top of the hill easily. There's a small ledge above me and using my arms, I heave myself on it then continue to scale up the side until I arrive at the top. I sit down on the peak and stare out at the ground below me. It looks so beautiful, so serene from up here, not dark and twisted and full of death like it really is. As if it's a completely different place with no vampires around, screeching and killing anything that gets into their path. If I use my imagination, I can almost picture life peaceful. What would that be like? To live in a peaceful world?

I shake my head and force my attention off the land to my surroundings nearby. The ground below me is fairly flat, but there are crevices that weave in and out of the surface that drops down. If it was dark, those crevices would be death traps. *Death. Sylas. He asked me to kill him and I didn't. I let him turn into a beast.*

"Stop thinking about it," I mutter to myself.

My palms are sweaty and covered with dirt, so I wipe them on my jeans to clean them off. There's a small rock on the ground next to my feet. I pick it up and throw it over the side of the cliff, watching it fall until it hits the bottom and breaks apart like I'm about to.

I can feel it. I can feel. My emotions are going haywire and I don't know how to turn them off. *God, what the hell do I do?*

"You need to turn off your emotions," Monarch tells me. "They will ruin you—what you need to do."

I watch as he urges a young boy behind the red door, pushing on his back. The boy refuses to go, though, and Monarch has to grab him and drag him in, his body leaving a trail of blood on the floor as he disappears into the room.

"What if I can't?" I ask Monarch as he stands in the doorway, wiping the blood off his hands onto his white coat. "What if I don't want to?"

He looks angry, but it's quickly replaced by calmness as he sighs. "I know that it's difficult, Kayla, but you have to remember it's for the greater good. The cruelties you suffer through will turn you into the strong person you need to become."

I know he's probably right, but it feels wrong. Still, even though it hurts, I bury the pain deep inside me; shove it down into a box and lock it away inside. Then I turn towards the red door, knowing what he wants me to do;

preparing to take my next victim because that's what will make me become a stronger person in the future.

The sound of rocks tumbling rips through the memory and my eyes fly open. Springing to my feet, I span my arms out to the sides and turn in a circle, searching the land and cliff for any movement. I can see nothing around other than dirt and rocks, so I brush the dirt off my pants then decide I should probably return to the others and stop running away from the problem.

I trek back to the edge of the rock so I can climb back down. Lowering my body, I get ready to jump off the ledge, knowing the fall won't hurt me. But as I'm about to bend my knees, I hear something.

Thump... Thump.

I pause and hear it again.

Thump... Thump.

I tense, crouched down, sensing some movement behind me. Someone or something is back there; something with a heartbeat. I spin around to the side as I hear the noise again, but I don't see anything. I whirl in the other direction and hear the thump again. It's coming from the side of me, down in one of the crevices in the rock.

I cautiously make my way over to the edge, keeping my senses on high alert. I can smell and taste the dirt, feel the heat of the air, feel my hyperawareness as I peer down into the crevice just over the edge.

The gap is rather deep and burrows down into the rock, but I can see movement in its shadows.

Thump...Thump... Thump... Thump.

The rhythm is steady and strong; I'm almost positive it's human. "Whoever you are, show yourself," I yell, my voice echoing down into the gap in the rock

Fear is radiating off them—I can feel it—and it makes me less afraid, if that makes any sense. I get down on my stomach and stick my head into the gap. "It's okay, I won't hurt you."

A girl's voice answers me, "How do I know that you aren't a monster trying to trick me?"

"If I was a monster, I'd be down in the shadows with you," I say, trying not to roll my eyes. "Not out in the sun. I wouldn't be talking to you, either." I scoot closer to the edge to try and get a better view of her.

"You have a point," she yells up to me. Rocks tumble down the hole as a figure starts to climb up the side through the shadows.

When she reaches the top, I grab her hand and pull her out of the hole. Standing up, I hoist her to her feet and out into the sun.

She's taller than me, although she's about my age. Her skin is tanner than mine and her hair is black and coiled into small strands that hang down from her head. She's wearing a dark shirt and pants, carrying a small pack on her back. Plus, in her hand is a sharp dagger, and when she gets her footing, she aims the tip at my throat.

"You lied. You're not human," she says warily. Her hand holding the dagger trembles. "What are you? And how do I know I can trust you?"

"You're right. I'm not human, but I'm not a vampire, either," I tell her, stepping away from the tip of the knife, even though I doubt she's going to use it on me. "But I did come from The Colony... there's actually several of us around." I pause, assessing her over. "Did you get thrown out of The Colony in The Gathering or have you been out for a while?"

She doesn't answer; instead she studies me for a moment. Then she relaxes as she lowers the dagger and puts it into the bag. "Sorry about that, but you can never be too careful." She pauses. "My name is Nichelle."

I don't give her my name. I'm too cautious of her. "You didn't answer my question. Did you just get sent up from The Colony?"

Her forehead creases. "No... I came from a town off in the distance." She points over her shoulder at the hills and desert behind her.

"A town? What? You mean another colony?" I have no idea what she's talking about. A town? Maybe she's insane.

She nonchalantly shrugs. "Town, Colony, I think they mean the same thing."

My jaw drops in shock because I can tell she's not lying—feeling she's telling the truth—which means Sylas was right; there are other colonies. *How many are there? And how can they survive out in this wasteland?*

"Hey, are you all right?" Nichelle asks, inching closer to me and snapping me out of my stupor.

"I'm fine," I tell her, but I'm still in shock. All this time there were other colonies. Are they better than the one

I lived in? Are there rules? "I just didn't realize that there were others besides us."

"It's hard to believe, huh?" She smiles and I'm not sure how to react to her cheerful demeanor. "The members of The Colony forget that there is a whole world out here with people and everything."

I'm silent for a while because I'm not sure what to say. This is so crazy. More colonies all this time and what if they're better? I open my mouth to say… well, something, but thunder suddenly claps as lightening blazes across the sky.

Seconds later, rain showers down, splashing against my face and soaking my hair. "Follow me. I know a place that'll keep us out of the rain." I motion Nichelle to follow me as I turn around and start to descend the cliffy hillside.

"Why are you here anyway?" I call out over the thunder as I maneuver myself over the edge of the rock and then drop down onto the ledge. Surprisingly, she easily slides down to the side of me.

"I am looking for someone," she tells me as our feet sink into the dirt and rocks. "A girl named Kayla. Maybe you know her?" she calls out over the rain, shielding her hand over her eyes.

I tense, but keep my composure, knowing better than to let her know who I am. Not until she tells me why she's here. "I think I know who she is. Why are you looking for her, though?"

She eyes me over with a questioning look. I start to wonder if she might know more than she's letting on; if she knows that I'm Kayla. "I'm here to help her," she says with a brief pause before continuing, "to help her save the world."

Chapter 5

For a second I don't think I've heard her right, but as I replay her words over and over again, I realize that I did.

But how does she know?

I jump down from the ledge and land gracefully on the loose ground below. Nichelle drops her pack, squats down and then swings her legs over the ledge. She grasps the edge then lowers her body slowly over until she's half way down and then lets go. She lands on her feet in the dirt beside me, her boots scuffing against the loose rocks.

"You seem comfortable moving around," I tell her, knowing it's a weird statement, but still. When Aiden was human he couldn't maneuver around like that. If I didn't know any better, I'd guess Nichelle was a Day Taker; however, she has a heartbeat.

She shrugs as she dusts the dirt and mud off her hands. "I have had years of training." She stretches her arm back up in the direction of the ledge and grabs her bag.

Training? "Are you a Bellator?" I ask her as I start to hike to the bottom of the slope.

She gapes at me as she puts her bag back on. "A what?"

"A Bellator... they were the people who trained at my Colony."

"Well, at my Colony, I'm called a Protector."

It seems the same to me, and the idea that they have titles at Nichelle's colony makes me question just how different hers is from mine, which makes me instantly put my guard up once more.

I try to keep quiet the rest of our journey down the hill. When I reach the bottom, I nod my head in the direction of the cave. "This way."

She follows me as rain continues to drench us and the grey sky lights up with silver blazes of lightning. We don't say a word to each other as we hike towards the cave. I'm getting tenser with every step, wondering if I should simply hit her over the head and knock her out to avoid any mishaps. However, before I can come up with a plan, Maci comes sprinting around the corner hill.

"Kayla!" she cries out. When she reaches me, she throws her arms around my waist. "I knew you didn't leave us." I stiffen because she just let out my secret; said my name. Before I can respond, Maci releases me and turns towards Nichelle. "And you found her."

"Yes, I guess I did," Nichelle says. I gape at Maci because it seems like she knows Nichelle.

"What do you mean, you found her?" I ask as the rain simmers down to a drizzle. "You knew Nichelle was looking for me?"

Maci nods her head up and down vigorously. "I did."

I never know how to react to Maci's strange behavior, so I don't respond. Instead, I lead her and Nichelle around the hill to the flat area just below the cave. By the time we get there, the rain has stopped, though the thunder and lightning still echo across the sky.

Greyson is sitting in the cave's entrance with a fire glowing beneath the shelter. He holds what looks like a dead lizard in his hand. He takes in Nichelle slowly as she and Maci follow me up the hill towards the cave.

Aiden and Tristan are right behind him, in the shadows of the cave, protecting themselves from the daylight that hides beneath the clouds and smoke. Aiden watches Nichelle suspiciously and then he finally steps out of the cave, drawing the hood of his jacket over his head and tucking his hands into the sleeves.

"Who is that?" He nods his head in Nichelle's direction.

I sigh as I keep climbing. "It's Nichelle. She says she's from... another colony." It sounds strange coming out of my mouth; I doubt anyone will believe me.

"There are no other colonies," Aiden argues, taking a step down the hill, his boots knocking wet rocks and chunks of mud down the slope. "If there were, we would know about them." Both him and Greyson eye Nichelle skeptically, their muscles raveled, edgy and on guard, which makes me uneasy.

Greyson stands to his feet, leaving the dead lizard on a rock. With his arms out to the side, he traipses down the hill to stop beside Aiden. "Aiden's right. If there are other colonies, then why haven't we known about them? It doesn't make any sense."

They take a few more steps towards us, meeting us at the center of the hill. Then Greyson and Aiden begin to circle around Nichelle with a dark look in their eyes like they're going to attack her or something.

I turn with them, not sure why I'm protecting Nichelle, other than she hasn't given me a reason not to. "Don't even think about doing anything to her."

Aiden pauses, his head slanting to the side. "Why not?"

"Because she hasn't done anything to us," I say with warning in my tone as I shoot him a look of caution. "And if you do make a move on her," I challenge, "then you have to go through me."

Aiden's eyes unexpectedly light up, as though he likes this idea, and I remember that this isn't the Aiden I first met. He starts to circle us again and Nichelle reaches to her side towards the leather pouch, taking out a small knife.

"I can protect myself," she says, aiming the knife out in front of her. "I don't need you to do it for me."

I shake my head and move with Aiden, making sure to keep myself between them at all times. "No, you can't. Trust me… he's a lot stronger than you."

"Yes, I can," she argues. "Strength doesn't outweigh skill."

"Yeah, let her try," Aiden insists with a look on his face that makes me want to slap him.

I probably would have, too, but Maci suddenly steps up between Aiden and me, tipping her chin up to look Aiden in the eye. "Nichelle's telling the truth, Aiden. I've seen where she comes from."

Aiden looks down at Maci with doubt. I seize the opportunity to leap forward, grabbing him by his jacket and shoving him backward, forcing him to stumble back into a large boulder on the hillside. "Stop it now. Just because you're suddenly strong, doesn't mean you need to be an asshole for no reason."

A glint of anger emerges in his eyes as he rises to his feet, his clothes muddy. The anger vanishes, though, as he shakes his head, and the old Aiden surfaces. "Sorry, I don't know what's got into me." He turns and heads back to the cave as if nothing happened. I am starting to think that I might have a real problem on my hands because Day Taker Aiden is very impulsive and erratic.

Greyson continues to watch Nichelle with interest, but he stops tormenting and circling her. "So, Nichelle, why haven't we seen you or any others from your colony before?"

I get where they're coming from... sort of, but I can feel Nichelle's telling the truth, so they need to back the hell down. "Greyson, I'd be able to tell if she is lying, and she's not."

Tristan's voice carries from over my shoulder. "Kayla's right. Nichelle's not lying. There are other people out there. The Highers just haven't found them yet."

We all turn in his direction. He's wearing a dark grey hoodie, the hood pulled over his head, and his hands tucked up in the sleeves. He crosses his arms with a stoic look on his face, staying in the shadows on the hill.

I step towards him with caution, rocks slipping down the hill. I have to put my hands on the ground to get my balance. "What do you mean the Highers haven't found them?" I question. "Are they looking for them? And how do you know this?"

"Of course the Highers are looking for them," he says, glancing at the land over my shoulder. "How else will they keep themselves in control if they allow other colonies to exist? The Highers are greedy and they want to control the entire world, so they've been tracking down other colonies and eliminating them."

I eye him over as I fold my arms. "How do you know all this?"

He shrugs. "Because you weren't the only reason I was sent out here." His blue eyes land on Nichelle. "The Highers also sent me to find others."

Before I can react, he leaps down the hill and smashes into Nichelle. Their bodies crash together and they fall to the ground, legs tangled, arms gripping onto each other as they tumble down the steep slope. Dirt flies up from the ground as they punch and hit each other, kneeing each other in the gut. Nichelle even gets a handful of Tristan's blond hair.

I dash down the hill after them as Nichelle lets out a shout and tries to take a swing at Tristan with her knife aimed out, but he knees her in the stomach and jumps on her, pinning her to the ground. He tips his head back with his hands around Nichelle's neck as she struggles to breathe, kicking her feet up at him.

"Tristan stop!" I cry out as I slide down the hill towards them. Nichelle's gasping for air as Tristan only tightens his hold. Before I can get to them, there's a loud grunt and then everything gets quiet as Tristan slumps over.

Oh God. I know before I reach them what has happened, but when I get there, I still feel a little shock. Tristan's body is on top of Nichelle, but not moving, and there's a pool of blood on the ground next to them. My hand tremors as I grab his shoulder and flip him over, not surprised to see Nichelle's knife sticking out of his chest.

Nichelle places her hands over her head and flips her body into a standing position. Reaching down, she pulls the knife from Tristan's chest and wipes the blood off on the sleeve of her shirt. Then, with zero emotion on her face, she tucks it back into her pouch.

"I'm sorry," she says. I can tell she's on guard, worried I might retaliate. "But he would have killed me if I didn't kill him first."

I'm taken aback by the fact that Tristan is dead. I feel the slightest bit of aching in my chest, especially when I stare down at him. Yes, he'd gone bad since he'd been put out into the Real World, yet at the same time, I can't forget the sweet, kind Tristan I knew in The Colony. Besides, he came back here and told Aiden about me being trapped in the cell. He's done both good and bad stuff, which makes me feel conflicted about his death. I'm not sure what to do, how to react, although I feel like ramming my fist into Nichelle's face.

"I'm sorry, Kayla," she says, her expression softening. "I really am, but in this world, you can't hesitate... it's a matter of life and death."

I understand that all too well, but I still can't speak. Staring down at Tristan's body, I struggle to sort through my thoughts on whether or not I should hurt Nichelle.

Nichelle walks back to Tristan's body and squats down beside him. She reaches over and gently closes Tristan's lifeless eyes then, standing back up, she glances over her shoulder at me.

"It wasn't his fault he was that way. He couldn't help that they changed him," she says softly.

"You knew what he was?"

She nods. "I could tell the second he spoke, but still... I wouldn't have killed him if I didn't have to." She walks up to me, stopping just short of me while she looks me straight in the eyes. "It's why we have to stop this; stop all the changing. It's time for people to be free instead of experiments. And you can do that, Kayla."

I glance over at Tristan and then back at Nichelle, knowing she's right, feeling it in my bones. I need to stop this; stop innocent people from getting hurt.

It's time to save the world.

Chapter 6

We—or rather I—decide I better do something with Tristan's body before darkness arrives. Maci wants to bury him, however I refuse to do it. Even the buried smell of death would attract the vampires and that's the last thing I need at the moment. I remember the ditch on the outskirts of the colony that Aiden and I jumped over the night before and it seems like a good place to take him. Aiden wants to go with me, but I tell him no because I don't trust him, and besides, he'll move too slowly in daylight. Deep down, though, I simply want to get away from it all for a while; clear my head.

I pick up Tristan's lifeless body and sling it over my shoulder, trying not to think about what I'm doing because it hurts my stomach when I do. Then I leave the cave and head out into desert where the sand has been dampened by the rain. The sky is starting to tinge orange on the other side of the clouds, which means the sun is lowering and nighttime will soon be here. I keep my pace quick and my footsteps light, knowing the last thing I want to do is be out at dark. Yes, vampires aren't a problem, but the abominations are.

After what seems like an eternity, I reach the ditch secluded just on the edge of the city limits and carefully lay Tristan's body down in the soft dirt. Then I do something really weird and I don't even know why, other than I fill some sort of finality in the moment. Without even thinking, I tenderly run my finger down his cheek as I remember the way he used to be, before the Highers got their hands on him and changed him; made him a killer and pawn to be used against good people. He was innocent. He could barely harm a thing and they had turned him into a monster.

I grow furious as I think about all the harm the Highers have caused. It is getting late and I am tempted to wait around to watch for the Highers, see if they come out to feed so I can try to pick them off one by one. However, as my temper subsides, I realize the only way to for me to seek revenge against them is to put an end to everything.

"Rationalize," Monarch whispers in my head. "Keep a level head and wait until it's time."

I want to tell him to shut up, remembering what happened back in Cell 7, but I'm not really sure if he's even talking in my head or if it's a memory. Plus, what he's saying seems right; I need to keep a level head. The Highers, vampires and the abominations all must go. The only way to do that is to find a cure and I'm the key to finding it. So, even though it kills me, I turn and head back to the cave.

***

When I get back, it's dark, which of course means the vampires are out, yelping and nipping at each other, their eyes dripping blood, their bodies decaying flesh. But they keep their distance from me, especially because I walk on top of the boulders; jumping from one to the other, making sure none of them follow me. Their cries echo through the night as I climb calmly up to the cave, quickly slipping inside before putting the rock in front of the entrance again.

It's darker inside, yet my night vision allows me to see everything clearly as I walk to the back, stooping low to avoid hitting my head on the section of the cave that dips downward. I can see where everyone is sleeping. Aiden, who is leaning up against the wall, has his eyes shut, although I'm fairly certain he's wide-awake, listening to me walk around.

I don't go to him, heading off in the opposite direction, instead, and step over Nichelle's leg that's stretched out.

"You can see in the dark?" Nichelle asks me quietly. "Either that, or you are a really good guesser of where everything is."

I sit down next to her on the dirt floor and lean against the rock wall behind me. "Yeah, I think maybe even better than I can in the daytime," I tell her, absentmindedly touching the side of my eyes with my hand, pressing down, wondering why I can see in the dark. Sure, it's because I'm a Day Taker, but how is it possible to see in the night. What makes it work?

Maci is cuddled next to her on the floor and I shake my head, trying not to smile. "It doesn't take her long to get attached to someone does it?" I ask.

"She's a good kid," Nichelle says.

"She really is," I agree with her.

"You two are close, aren't you?" she asks, sitting up carefully so she doesn't wake up Maci.

I shake my head, but it feels like a lie. "I'm not close to anyone really." Thoughts of what Monarch has always said, rips into my head. *You need to turn off your emotions. They will ruin you; what you need to do.*

Before she can say anything else, I change the subject because this particular one is pissing me off. "How about you explain why the hell you came out here to look for me?"

"Because I was told this is where I could find you; at least people who used to belong to your colony... I'm supposed to take you back with me to our town." She pauses, considering something. "There's a man there. Mathew. He's probably the oldest person in town. He says he has things he needs to tell you. Things that may be able to help you save humanity."

"I don't understand how someone I don't even know could know about me," I say. "It doesn't make any sense."

"Oh, you know him. You probably just don't remember him." She yawns. "He was a doctor a long time ago, but there were things being done he didn't approve of, so he left and went out on his own."

I listen to the steadiness of her heart beating and it lets me know what she says is true, or at least that she believes it's true. I do remember there were a lot of doctors in white coats experimenting on me all the time when I was younger.

She suddenly reaches out in the darkness and grabs my arm. My initial reaction is to jerk away, but for some reason I don't. "Kayla, you have to trust me. I need you to come back with me before it's too late."

"What do you mean before it's too late?" I ask, glancing between her hand and her expression, which is filled with panic.

She pulls her hand away and sighs. "Mathew was bit by a vampire a few days ago."

"If he was bit he would have either died or turned into one by now." I know I should be more sympathetic; however sympathy isn't really one of my traits.

"Normally, that's true, but when Mathew was first involved with the doctors from your colony, he used some of the injections that they were experimenting with on himself." She pauses for a moment, choosing her words carefully. "Although he's not immune, one of the shots did cause a delay in his transformation..." She sucks in a deep breath and her heart trembles. "He... he believes that it's part of the cure."

I take in everything she just told me. If what she says is correct, I need to talk to this Mathew, but do I dare go to this place? It's unknown.

"Follow your instincts," Monarch whispers. *"They'll never lead you astray."*

I hesitate for a moment before I respond. "Okay, I'll go just as soon as daylight hits." I feel lost, knowing I can only hope I'm making the right choice. "Now get some sleep. I need to make sure that you have enough energy to get us there."

"Thank you, Kayla," she says softly then lies down on the dirt floor and closes her eyes.

Seconds later, she falls asleep and I sort of envy her for being able to. I sit wide awake, listening to the vampire cries right outside as I wonder if I've made the right choice while, at the same time, knowing that time is running out.

Chapter 7

Because I no longer need to sleep, I just sit, listening to the breathing of those around me and watching the entrance to the cave until morning comes. My only company in the darkness is the shrieks of the vampires from outside.

I'm pretty sure Aiden was listening to my conversation with Nichelle during the night, but he has stayed quiet in his corner and hasn't budged since we quit talking, leaving me alone with my thoughts.

Eventually, the shrieks of the vampires begin to fade, and I assume that the day is starting to break, so I stand up from my seat on the floor of the cave. Raising my arms up above me, I stretch my stiff limbs, preparing for my journey. The rest of the group starts to stir as I walk over to the cave entrance and roll back the rock that covers it, letting the sunlight spill in the entrance of the cave.

I step outside, staring at the vacant land while breathing in the fresh air, wondering if there will ever be a time when people can look at the view when the sky is dark.

"So you're simply going to leave with Nichelle and abandon the rest of us?" Aiden asks, walking up behind me. I know he's angry at me because I'm leaving, because I trust Nichelle and because I won't tell him that I love him when he wants me to. Desperately.

I turn around and look at him; I mean *really* look at him. He has his jacket wrapped around him, his hood over his head and his hands tucked in the sleeves. I can barely see his face in the shadows, but I can tell he's upset and I feel sorry for him. He didn't want to change into what he is now, but he did it because he thought it was the only way to save me. He cares for me that much. I'll never feel the same way about him, though. At least, I don't think I can.

I don't know why I do it, other than it feels like an impulse, as well as the right thing to do. I reach up and gently touch his cheek, causing his body to shudder. "I have to go, Aiden. This Mathew may know the answers to finding a cure."

His eyes soften. "I thought you and I had the answers up here," he taps the side of his head, "locked away in our memories."

I sigh and remove my hand from his cheek. "We're supposed to. The papers that Sylas and I found might have had what we needed to help us, but they're lost and this may be the only chance we have to save the world."

"And what if you're wrong."

"Then at least I tried."

Nichelle walks out of the cave, ready to go, her pack slung over her shoulder. Her hair is pulled up behind her head and she has a jacket tied around her waist. She glances back and forth between Aiden and I with a curious look on her face.

"You ready to go, Kayla?"

I nod, watching Aiden as he backs away from me, his eyes glinting with rage as he stares at Nichelle. There it is again. The anger. Something I never really saw in him before he changed. When he notices me staring at him, he pauses, his lips parting like he's going to say something, but Maci and Greyson step out of the cave and he snaps his mouth shut.

Greyson is carrying what little gear the group has and Maci skips over to the side of me, her red hair blowing in the breeze.

"Are we ready?" she asks me, her eyes sparkling with excitement.

I'm confused. "Umm... Maci, you aren't coming with us."

She looks at me with a smug expression on her face; it throws me back a little. "Yes, I am."

I glance over to Nichelle, who shrugs her shoulders. "I didn't tell her she could go."

I crouch down in front of Maci so we're eye-level. "I know you want to come, but it'll be faster if I go alone with Nichelle."

She shakes her head in protest. "No, I'm going."

I glance over to Aiden for help, but he aims the same smug look at me and I can tell that I'm going to have to fight this battle on my own.

Sighing, I stand back up and pat her on the head. "Somebody has to take care of Aiden. If he goes into the sunlight, it'll hurt him. I need you to take care of him. And Greyson, too. Do you think you can do this for me?"

She looks as though she is buying into my little story. "Okay, I think I can do that."

Then Aiden walks out of the shadows of the cave and doesn't stop until he's right in my face. "This is bull shit," he says, his anger there again, burning like a fire. "If you're going, we're all going with you."

"You can't," I start to argue, knowing if they all go, then I'm going to be stuck worrying about them. Plus, they'll slow us down.

"Watch me," he says and then he turns to Nichelle. "Which way is it?"

Nichelle eyes him over, as if she doesn't trust him, but then she turns and starts walking up the hill. "Follow me," she says, motioning him to follow.

Maci smiles at me and then takes my hand, pulling me along. "See, Kayla, I told you I was going."

I shake my head, trying not to smile as I follow her because it's not funny. She shouldn't be going. It's too dangerous, yet the fact that she said she was going and now she is, is sort of amusing.

It makes me wonder what else she can see. I think about asking her if we're going to be okay, but when I really think about it, I'm not sure that I want to know the answer.

Chapter 8

The journey across the sandy desert land is slow, hot and it irks me to know that, if I was traveling it solo, I could have made it to the city and back by now. I drift to the back of the group, checking to make sure no one is getting left behind as we all trudge farther towards the unknown. Nichelle leads the way across the desert land; her bag on her shoulder, her back hunched over like she's tired. Maci is quiet, looking exhausted and hungry, but I can tell she's trying not to complain. Aiden's quiet, too, as he walks just in front me with his head tucked down, trying to keep the light from hitting his face.

Aiden has been acting a bit more strange the more and more time goes by. I know that he has changed into a Day Taker, but still, something else doesn't seem quite right about him. The mood swings… I don't remember being that moody.

I watch him from the corner of my eye as I wind around sagebrush and cacti while sand gets in my eyes because of the dry breeze. He still has his hood up and hands covered, but strangely, he doesn't seem drained of energy the way Sylas and Tristan were when they traveled in the daylight. I stare at him a moment longer, wondering what feels off, but I'm unable to put my finger on it. When he glances at me, I quickly avert my attention from him and focus on clouds of dust the breeze is kicking up.

The sky grows darker with every step we take, and when we reach the edge of a hill, readying to wind down, Nichelle pauses for a moment, waiting for the rest of us to catch up with her.

She looks up at the darkening sky with her hand shielded over her eyes, and her face masks with concern. "I don't think we're going to make it back to town before darkness falls."

"How much further is it?" Greyson asks as he wipes some sweat off his forehead with the back of his hand. His skin is sweaty and stained with dirt and he looks exhausted.

Nichelle points at the desert land before us. "It's over there."

I step next to her and track where she's pointing. There's a deep basin that stretches out a few miles and I can see a small speck on the other side. It looks different than the land I'm used to; more green.

"How long will it take to get there?" I ask Nichelle, measuring up the distance while knowing if it were just me I could be there in a flash.

"Normally," she looks around at our group, "well, I'd be there already. But we are moving at a much slower pace than I'm used to, so I'm not sure."

I nod, understanding what she means. "Is there somewhere nearby that we can stop for the night?" I ask when, really, what I want to do is take off and let everyone else stay behind for the night.

Nichelle scans the area below us for someplace to hide as I hear the screeching of the very first vampires awakening for the night. Everyone grows uneasy, restless, as they glance around at the shadows on the hills, the desert land, and the caves in the sides of the hills. So many places for vampires to be hiding and they could walk out at any moment.

Maci starts to shake with nerves and leans in close to me. "Kayla, I'm scared."

I pat her head. "Everything will be okay. I promise."

Nichelle twists one of the coils of her hair with her fingers as she deliberates then her eyes light. "I think I may know of a place. If we hurry, we can make it before it gets completely dark."

I nod and then we take off in a line down a small trail that weaves down into the basin, Nichelle taking the front and me taking the back. The trail is narrow and drops off sharply on one side towards jagged rocks and cliffs. I try to keep an eye on everyone as we hike down towards the bottom, having to catch Maci more than a few times.

It's getting darker, the sky a deep grey, making it difficult for them to see. The trail begins to slope further towards the ground and Maci has to brace into the rocky wall beside us to keep her balance.

"Be careful," Nichelle whispers from up ahead, motioning us to keep going. "We're are almost there. Everyone keep moving."

I see the edge of the ledge where Nichelle seems to be heading and relief washes over me because everyone is making me nervous. It's too stressful traveling with the group and I wish I were alone.

Suddenly, Maci stumbles, and when I reach out to grab her, she slips from my grasp, tumbling over the edge of the cliff. She shouts my name as she falls, and I cry back at her. My eyes widen as I rush to the edge and look down.

"Maci!" I shout towards the bottom, lying flat on my stomach as I peer down over the edge. I spot her a ways down, lying at the bottom on the rocks. She's not moving. I feel a flicker of panic, one I'm not used to as the others rush over to the side of me. It hurts, knowing she's down there, helpless and in pain.

I need to get to her. Now.

"What happened?" Nichelle asks, rushing up to me.

"Maci slipped and fell over the edge." I look down at the ground below, panicking more than I ever have before. What if she's not okay? What if she's gone? "I'm going to climb down." I push up and swing my legs around to climb down to the rocks below.

Greyson grabs my arm, stopping me. He's afraid. Scared of what may happen if we don't find somewhere to hide from the vampires soon. "Kayla, that was a long fall—" A vampire lets out a cry and he jumps, more afraid as he glances around with worry. "We need to get to a safe place, quick."

I shrug his hand off and lower my feet over the edge. "Then go. I can get Maci by myself."

Aiden steps up in front of me when I'm halfway over the side. "Wait."

"Why?" Dirt and rocks scratch at my palms, but I barely feel it.

"I'm going with you," he says, crouching down in front of me. "You might need some help."

"I need you to go with Nichelle and Greyson," I say, pushing my way back up over the ledge, holding my weight on my arms, my feet hanging below me. He starts to argue, but I cut him off. "First of all, I'm the only one in this group that is immune from the vampires. It makes no sense for the rest of you to risk yourselves." I lower my voice. "And I need you to help watch the others in case the vampires try to attack them."

He shakes his head, annoyed. Cries echo around us, multiplying as more and more vampires wake up.

"I'll hurry and get Maci then meet up with you guys." I look over at Nichelle. "Can you tell me where the hiding spot is?"

She squats down in front me. "Just stay on the trail and when you get to the bottom there's a large rock to the right. There's a trail hidden behind it that leads to the side of a hill that has several caves in it. I think one of them may be large enough for all of us to climb in until morning." She stands back up and dusts the dirt off her hands.

"Okay, I'll be there as soon as I can," I tell her, unsure how true that really is, especially because I'll be bringing Maci back with me.

She starts to walk away, but stops and reaches into the leather pouch, pulling out a knife. "You may need this." She hands it to me.

I balance my weight on one arm and take it from her, slipping it into my back pocket; ready to go, ready to get to Maci. Help her. She needs my help.

Aiden moves closer to me, still seeming pissed. "I don't like leaving you alone."

He's getting on my nerves and slowing me down from getting to Maci. "I'll be fine, now go."

He reluctantly stands up as the rest of them head off down the trail in a line. I lower my feet, pressing my boots to the side of the hill, then dig my fingers into it and rapidly scale down the side like a lizard.

When I finally plant my feet on the bottom, I rush over to Maci's side and kneel down, feeling sick to my stomach at the sight. She's lying face down in the dirt; her arm is kinked at a weird angle, a bone protruding through the skin. Blood drips down her arm, forming a small pool of blood around her and the rocks below her.

I lean down and listen to see if she's breathing. I hear her take a breath, but it's small and weak. Still, I let out a sigh, relief swelling within me because at least she's still breathing; she's alive.

"Maci, can you hear me?"

She lets out a groan, her eyes opening up. "Kayla?"

"It's going to be okay." It feels like I'm lying to myself, though.

She tries to push herself up, but gasps from the pain and drops back down to the ground, her face twisted in pain

"Kayla, is that you?" Her voice is quiet and shaky, her hair is covered in dirt and fragments of rocks and her shirt's stained with blood.

I need to help her. Somehow. Get her out of here and heal her.

As I'm figuring out what to do, I hear what sounds like approaching footsteps coming from behind me. I whirl around and scan the black land and rocks behind me, but I don't see anything. Still, I'm running out of time. Vampires will be here soon, especially when they catch the scent of blood.

"Maci, can you move at all?" I ask, gently trying to help her turn over.

"I think so, but I need some help. It hurts." She's on the verge of tears.

"Hold on, okay… I'm going to roll you over, but you need to try and be quiet. Don't scream." She nods and then I place my hands under her arms and vigilantly roll her to the side.

She bites down on her lip and winces, stopping herself from crying out as the pain gets to her. I can smell the blood and it worries me, especially because she has more wounds than I thought. There's a large gash across her forehead that looks fairly deep, blood is streaming down her cheek. I rip a piece of fabric from the bottom of my shirt and tie it around her head to try and slow the bleeding down. Then I unwrap my jacket from around her waist and gently wrap her broken arm with it. I take the sleeves of the jacket and loop them around her neck then tie them in the back, securing her arm against her chest.

Her eyes start to drift shut. That worries me as well.

"Maci, you need to keep your eyes open," I say. She blinks at me. "We need to find a way to get you out of here..." I look for the best way out. Vampires have emerged and are crossing the land. Everywhere. There's only one option and that's up. Dammit. "Maci, you're going to have to climb onto my back and hold onto me with one arm, so we can get out of here. We're going to have to hurry, okay?" I'm not even sure she can do it, but I have to try.

She nods and I turn around, putting my back towards her. She reaches around my neck with her good arm and grasps onto me, her grip weak.

"Now make sure you hold on tight, okay?" I sense how scared she is and how much pain she's in. I can also feel her starting to fade. I put my hands behind my back so I can hold onto her legs then freeze when I see movement in front of us.

A group of vampires, salivating from the mouth and bleeding from the eyes, creep out of the shadows of the rocks around us. Their flesh is peeling, their eyes hungry as they snap their teeth, surrounding us. I need to get out of here. Now.

"Hold on tightly," I tell Maci and then, with one swift spring on my toes, I launch myself onto the rock, only letting her go at the last second.

She grips onto me, but I can feel her grip loosening as her arm begins to slide from around my neck. I dig one set of my fingers deep into the rock, feeling it scrape at my flesh, but I don't feel pain since I quickly heal. Then I push my boots against the surface, baring my weight on them, before I move my other arm around my back to hold onto her legs tightly. The vampires shriek, overlapping the sounds of thudding as they ram their bodies against the cliff side. The teeth of one graze my boots and I lose my balance. We start to slip back down the hill, I plunge my fingers and toes deeper into the rock and manage to get us to a stop just before we reach the vampires. I begin to scale up again when one of their rotten hands wraps around my ankle. I slam my boot into its face, but it continues to keep hold of me, dragging me downward, sniffing the air with the scent of Maci's blood. It won't let go.

I search frantically for an escape; some way out of this where they won't devour Maci. There's a lip on the rock nearby and I start to claw sideways towards it, while the vampire works to pull me down, using my body like a tug-o-war rope, but I manage to get my top half over to it.

"Maci, climb on it," I shout.

She shakes her head, holding onto me tighter. "No, I'm too scared."

The vampire jerks on my leg again, but I keep ahold of the rock. "Maci, please. I know your brave and I need you to do this for me, otherwise this is going to end badly."

She pauses then I feel her hold loosen. She shifts and begins rolling onto the lip. I hear her groan, but I don't have time to see if she's okay. It's time to kill, so I let go.

Falling into the midst of the howls and decaying flesh, I land gracefully on my feet, and with one swift movement, I retrieve Nichelle's knife that she's given me. I waste no time, slicing the face of the first one I come across. It howls out into the night and then the rest of them start to hover away, my scent frightening them as they deliberate whether to flee or feed. They inhale the air, blood dripping from their wounds. Their backs are hunched over and one of them dares to take a nip at me. I realize the scent of Maci's blood is overriding their fear, and without much more hesitation, they charge.

Their eyes bleed as they snap their jaws at me. A rounded, tall one with bulging eyes dives at me with its teeth out. I drop kick it in the face effortlessly and slam it into the ground, quickly sticking my knife into its body. It explodes into dust. The other ones are hesitant again as they watch. I bare my fangs, snapping my teeth at them. They pace around me as I spin in a circle with the knife out in front of me. Then they start to cower back towards the sand stretching across the land which is blanketed with darkness.

I start to relax when Maci's scream pierces the night. I quickly spin around and look up. Two vampires are mere inches away from her, crawling up the side, heading to-wards the lip in the cliff. I sprint over to the cliff and, with a spring, lunge upward, crashing into one of them. Holding onto their back, I reach around as it bites at me and plunge the knife into its chest. It bursts into dust and I quickly reach out to grab hold of the cliff's side as the other one continues to scale up towards Maci. I grab hold of its foot and jerk on its leg, forcing it downward. Then I let go and watch it fall and splatter against the rocks below.

I begin to breathe freely again when I notice shadows below me. At least a dozen vampires have returned. Blood rivers from their eyes and bits and pieces of flesh hang loosely off their bodies. They start to climb up the rock, filled with excitement as they stare at Maci. Drops of blood drip down from their mouths, dribbling from their chins as they focus solely on feeding. I use myself as a barricade in front of Maci as they swiftly reach us and then slash one by one with the knife, cutting flesh, nicking bone, spilling blood.

I try to protect her, but slowly, I begin to become overrun by them. They're everywhere. It seems as if there is no end to them. I continue to hold my knife, though, stabbing each of them in their hearts, spreading dust everywhere, refusing to go down without a fight. Their teeth nip toward my body, trying to rip into my flesh; some of them pulling away at the last second when they get a whiff of my scent. I throw my leg out and push them back, watching them stumble over each other as they fall to the ground, yet more keep coming up; climbing and climbing, hungry, seeking blood.

They start to cover my bottom half, coating my legs with bites. I've always had confidence in my fighting ability, but I begin fear this may be the end and poor Maci, she'll die with me.

As darkness and bites cover over me, I hear the sound of rocks tumbling down the hill above me. I try to flip around, ready to stab the predator, however my hand stops in mid-air when I see the figure of someone I know.

Aiden.

He pauses on the cliff just above us and grabs onto my wrist. "Relax, it's just me." He holds onto my hand as he looks at the piles of vampires below me, hanging onto me, covering the rocks around us and the land. "What do you think? Can we take them all?" he tries to joke

I shake my head as my body is jerked down. I turn around to see a nasty vampire, scaling up my body towards my face. It's missing half of its face and its eyes are full of hunger. Aiden retrieves his knife, ready to slash it when suddenly the vampire takes a whiff of the air. It freezes, looking straight at Aiden, and then it throws its head back and cries out.

The rest of them freeze and then together cry out.

I tense inside at the sight of it. Sheer terror on the faces that were just *causing* sheer terror.

The vampires quickly turn away from us, releasing my body and then flinging themselves to the ground, fleeing into the night while trampling over one another.

Once the land is cleared out, I gape up at Aiden who is staring at me, confused.

"What the hell just happened?" he asks, holding onto the cliff face with one hand as he gawks out at the land.

I stare at him in disbelief, my jaw hanging open. "I think you just scared them off."

He scratches his head, but doesn't look fazed. "Huh, who would have thought?"

I shake my head, still stunned. Aiden can walk with the vampires, just like me.

Chapter 9

"Monarch must have made you like me," I tell him, but I'm not sure if that's right or not. I'm only guessing, just like I have with everything else.

"You think?" he asks with a crook of his brow.

My shoulders rise and fall as I shrug. "I'm not sure... I wish I had better answers, but I don't, and I don't know how to get them. Hopefully, this new colony will." I rotate towards Maci, who's resting on the lip of the rock, and maneuver my way over to her.

Once I get up there, I lean down and scan her over for bite marks. "Are you okay? You didn't get bit, did you?"

She's curled in a ball and looks terrified to death with her arms cradled against her. She shakes her head, a faint smile on her face. "No bites. You kept them all away, Kayla; you saved me just like I knew you would."

I smile back at her, but it's difficult after what happened, not just with the vampires, but also with Aiden.

Aiden starts to climbs over to me and then lands beside us on the ledge. "Is she okay?"

I nod. "Yeah, for now."

"We should get going in case they come back." His voice is full of confusion as he stares out at the dark, silent land in front of us. I remember the first time the vampires ran away from me and I felt the same way. That something had to be wrong and they'd come back at any moment to finish me off.

I move to let Maci hop up on my back, but Aiden gently pushes me out of the way. "Let me carry her up."

I shake my head. "No, you don't have any of her blood on you. I'll carry her in case any vampires come back. At least your scent may chase them off."

He runs his fingers through his dark hair, sweeping strands out of his face, frustrated, then moves away and nods. "Okay, but I'm not sure if I really believe it's me that sent them running, just so you know, so don't blame me if they come back and decide they want to eat us."

"Okay," I say and then turn so Maci can crawl up on my back. She does so with a struggle, although she does manage to get on and hold tightly.

Aiden grows quiet as he gets lost in his own thoughts and turns in the direction the vampires ran away. Then, looking torn, he returns to the cliff's side and starts to climb up. I follow, moving a little slower, though I make it up to the top then move Maci to my arms and carry her so she doesn't have to hold her weight. Aiden leads us through the darkness down the trail that dips into the rocks, leading us toward the cave.

It's silent the entire way, but I'm edgy at every shadow and movement. Eventually we arrive at a cluster of large rocks blocking the path and Aiden climbs up and then drops down. I follow, landing a little loudly. There's rocks surrounding the area and Aiden rolls the largest rock out of the way, revealing a cave nestled behind it. I carry Maci inside. There isn't much room and when we enter it, it makes the fit even tighter, yet we somehow manage and Aiden seals us in with the rock.

I hear footsteps and spot Greyson and Nichelle moving up towards us as I set Maci down upon the floor.

"Is Maci okay? Is she hurt?" Greyson asks, flipping on a flashlight.

"She'll be all right, I think," I reply, though I'm not so sure. "Her arm's broken, and she has some cuts and gashes." I pause then glance at Aiden who's leaning against the cave wall. "We were attacked by a herd of vampires."

Greyson gapes as he shines the light onto Maci, curled up on her side with her hair blocking her face. "Did she get bitten?"

"No," I reply and look back at Aiden, wondering what he's thinking, wondering how he knew to come back to us. "But if Aiden hadn't shown up when he did then... well, I don't think we would have made it back."

He looks back at me with a confident grin on his face. "Only because I'm a badass." His weird behavior instantly returns, leaving me again wondering what's causing it. If it's just the Day Taker blood in him or maybe something else.

Chapter 10

We manage to make it through the rest of the night without any more vampire incidents, but for some reason, I feel like something bad is waiting for us in the near future. I can't figure out what, though. Maybe it's because I have trust issues. Or that every new place I've gone to something bad has happened. Like Cell 7. I was trapped. Sylas was bitten. God, Sylas.

It hurts to even think about him being out there either dead or running around with his flesh rotting off. I promised I'd kill him before it happened, but I didn't. I failed him.

Small slivers of light gleam through the cracks in the cave, announcing morning breaking through. Aiden removes the rock and light pours into our small hideout. Everyone is tired and hungry, and I know we need to get to the colony soon.

I glance at Maci, her eyes are still closed and she keeps moaning in her sleep.

"We should get going," I say as Nichelle picks up her pack.

"I agree, the sooner we get there, the quicker Maci will get the help that she needs," she says as she crawls out of the hole with her fingers hitched through her pack.

I place my hands underneath Maci's body and pick her up in my arms. Her eyes don't open and another moan escapes from her lips as I carry her out of the cave and into the light.

"How's she doing?" Nichelle asks as she places a light kiss on Maci's cheek. "She feels kind of warm. Are you sure she didn't get bitten?"

"I'm sure," I answer as Greyson and Aiden walk out behind us. Greyson stretches his arms above his head and yawns. Aiden has his hood over his head and his hands tucked up into his sleeves, watching me like a hawk for some reason. "I checked her over and there are only the cuts and a broken arm."

For some reason it looks like she doesn't believe me, however she still leads the way downhill and back to the main trail we were on the night before while the rest of us follow her. We hike down the curvy path for an hour or two until I finally see the small area that looks like a town off in the distance hidden in desert hills. There are buildings as well as paths, and I can see people moving around the border of it. I think, up until now, I wasn't one hundred percent convinced it really existed. Yet there it is; all green in the center of a lot of brown sand sitting below the hazy sky, although it looking at it does make the sky seem less hazy.

As we get nearer, I notice that there are a few bits and pieces of green popping up through the ground. I find it fascinating. I haven't seen any signs of life for a long time. At least I can't remember seeing any, but there it is, right in front of me, so different from the ground my colony is hidden underneath.

Aiden watches me while I trek up the trail with my eyes fixed on the scenery. "You know you could let me carry her for a while." He nods his head at Maci in my arms. "I won't bite her or anything."

"I know you wouldn't bite her," I tell him, "She's not heavy. Besides, she saved me once and I promised myself I'd do everything I could to protect her."

His eyes soften from below his hood. "You really care for her, don't you?"

"If caring means that I feel responsible, then yeah, I do." I jump over a rock in the path, landing on top and then leaping down while continuing to be careful not to drop Maci.

Aiden catches up with me, flying above for a few seconds as he jumps to the ground. He lands in the dirt effortlessly then glances over at Greyson and Nichelle just in front of us. In a lowered voice, he says, "So have you mentioned what happened last night to them?" He nods his head towards Greyson and Nichelle.

"You mean how the vampires were afraid of you?" I keep my eyes on the ground as the trail rises to a slope that ascends over a hill while bending my knees and keeping my balance.

"Yeah… I'm not sure I want to tell anyone until we can figure out why or if Monarch made me this way," he whispers, seeming uneasy.

"Don't worry, I haven't told them anything, but I'm pretty sure Monarch made you this way. It had to be him."

"What makes you so sure? They may have just left because they were afraid of you, like they usually do."

I hesitate for a moment, deciding whether I want to share my memory with him, and finally decide that he needs to know what Monarch told me about him. "Because of a memory I had about Monarch. I remember him telling me that you were the only other one like me, except—you were broken."

"Broken?" As his voice rises, Nichelle and Greyson glance back at us. He smiles at them as they look away puzzled then he leans in and lowers his voice. "What do you mean, broken?"

"He never told me how you were broken or why," I answer, working to keep my steps light at I walk around a few small rocks in the way. "He just said that you were."

"Well, that's great," he mutters. "I'm broken, but you don't know how."

"Sorry, maybe I shouldn't have told you."

"Yeah, maybe… or maybe not… I don't know."

"You don't know what?"

He shrugs. "I don't know anything anymore. Everything's changed—I've changed. And it makes figuring out what I want hard."

I'm not sure what to say, so I turn my head and look ahead, focusing on getting to the colony. I just about slam into the back Greyson and Nichelle who have suddenly stopped.

I look up, wondering what happened, but when I see Nichelle's apologetic face, I realize that something's wrong. But before I can set Maci down and get my knife, a net is thrown over the top of Aiden and I. Seconds later, a needle is jabbed into the side of my neck. I let out a gasp as my arms go limp, my body falling, falling, falling. Everything begins to blur and the last thing I see are a set of pale eyes peering down at me.

A Higher.

Chapter 11

My eyes are heavy and I struggle to open them. It feels like I'm moving, although I can't remember why. Then it all starts to come back to me in bits and pieces until suddenly I remember that I was betrayed.

I jerk my eyes open, panicking as I realize I'm lying on a cot in a room surrounded by brick walls. I slowly lift up my arms, wanting to move, but they feel like lead.

I glance around. There are no windows anywhere; only a large, metal door on the wall farthest from me and a pile of bricks in the corner, the ceiling is leaking something grimy.

Aching from head to toe, I sit up and stumble away from the cot making my way over to the door and try to pry it open.

Locked, of course.

Dammit. What is going on?

I'm pretty sure that I saw a Higher before I was sedated. *But why?* I know Nichelle wasn't lying when she told me her story about why I needed to come with her. So why do they have me locked up? And where are the others being kept?

Pacing back and forth, I feel the tension inside me begin to coil, knowing I need to get out of this of this place. I glance over at the door and center all of my strength on it. Backing up I run forward, ramming my body into it as hard as I can. Pain shoots throughout my body and the door doesn't budge. The only visible damage is a small dent from where my shoulder connected with it.

I rub my shoulder and let out a frustrated sigh, smashing my fist into the brick wall over and over again until bits and pieces crumble. I stomp back over to the cot and flop onto it. Folding my arms across my chest as I silently wait to see what will come next because it feels like everything is out of my hands now. I'm supposed to save the world, yet I can't even control what's going on around me.

A few minutes tick by and then I hear the lock on the door click. Nichelle enters wearing black pants and a shirt with her hair pulled back. She looks like she's cleaned up, smiling at me as she shuts the door.

"Hi, Kayla." She acts as if she's innocent and hasn't done anything wrong.

Anger fires through me and I hop off the cot and storm towards her, ready to beat the shit out of her. "Don't 'hi, Kayla' me."

She pulls out a long knife and aims it out in front of her. "Relax and let me explain."

I stop a few feet in front of her, eyeing the knife in her hand, knowing I could stop her from stabbing me if I really wanted to. "Explain what? How you lied to us; tricked us into believing you, only to lock us up?"

She keeps her knife pointed out at me and steps back, putting a bit of space between us. "That's not how it is. Locking you up was only a precaution to make sure that there's no chance that any of you would attack our people."

I know she is telling me what she believes is the truth, but I'm still skeptical. Plus, I'm still not over the fact that she stabbed me with a needle. "If that's true, then why did I see a Higher with you earlier?"

Her brows dip. "A Higher? I'm not sure what you mean. There are no Highers here."

Anger consumes me. I ball my hands into fists. "I saw him before I was injected and knocked unconscious."

She shakes her head and opens her mouth, ready to speak, but we're interrupted when the door creaks open and a man walks in. His hair is white like the outer part of ash, he has creases in his skin and his clothes looks old. He carries a stick that he leans on, as he hobbles as if it's hard for him to walk, yet his pale eyes make me wonder if it's all a trick.

I've lost all my trust, and in a flash, I lunge forward, snatching the knife from Nichelle's hand quickly skittering around her. Then, I dive for the Higher, grab his arm, and twist it behind him as I move around him, putting the blade to his throat.

He drops his stick in a panic. "Oh, no."

"Kayla, no!" Nichelle shouts with her hands out in front of her. "*Please*, don't hurt him."

The Higher tips his head back to look at me and I'm surprised by his fearless expression. "Well done, Kayla. Monarch has turned you into exactly what he had hoped for."

I press the knife closer to his throat, but he still keeps calm. "Then you know that I'm not afraid to use this to finish you off."

"I'm sure you aren't, but I'm not a Higher," he says evenly. "I'm just an old man that was bitten a long time ago."

I don't want to believe him, yet my little gift lets me know that he is telling the truth, even though it's confusing the shit out of me—everything is. "*What* are you then? You have the eyes of a Higher."

Nichelle inches closer to us, her hands still out in front of her, her movements calculated and cautious. "Kayla, please put the knife down. This is Mathew and he's here to help you."

Mathew motions his hands at Nichelle, ushering her back. "It is okay, Nichelle. Kayla has a good reason to not trust us. We didn't exactly give her and her friends the best welcome, did we?"

A trickle of blood runs down his throat from where the blade is pressing into his skin. With reluctance, I remove the knife from his neck and back away, letting him go. I have my answer; if he really were a Higher, he would not be bleeding, he would heal. I shove him over next to Nichelle and she catches him in her arms.

"Both of you better explain where my friends are and what is going on," I demand.

Nichelle shoots me a glare as she examines Mathew's neck while he fights to get his footing. "Are you okay?" she asks him and he nods.

Nichelle still checks the wound then pulls out a cloth from her pocket and hands it to him. Mathew takes the cloth as he picks up the stick and puts his weight against it. Then he presses cloth tightly over the wound to stop it from bleeding.

As I watch them, I can tell that there is a bond between the two of them, almost like Nichelle treats Mathew as if he is her father.

"You are good at what you do," he says to me. "And I'll explain everything I know. But first, how about I take you to the rest of your friends? I'm sure that they're just as anxious to see you as you are to see them."

Again, I know he speaks the truth, but for some reason, I feel wary. Still, having no other choice, I nod and follow him out the door with the knife clutched in my hand, not ready to fully trust them just yet.

Chapter 12

They take me down a hallway and into a large room, keeping close to me like they think I'm going to run or something. Inside the room sits a wooden table with chairs down both sides of it. There are no windows and the only light comes from the candles placed sporadically about, the flames flickering and dancing.

Leaning his weight on his stick, Mathew limps to the end of the table and takes a seat. He motions for me to take a seat next to him as he sets the stick down on the ground. "Please, have a seat."

I waver, looking around at the empty room while hovering near the door. "I thought you said we were going to meet the others?" I still have the knife, holding it out to my side, and Mathew eyes it with interest.

"You have nothing to worry about it, Kayla. It's okay to put the knife away; we aren't going to hurt you." He smiles at me as he crosses his arms on the table. "I've sent for someone to bring your friends here."

I plaster a fake smile on. "I think I'll simply hold onto it, just in case." I select a spot at the table a ways away from him and pull out a chair, sinking down into it. Nichelle goes to the opposite side of the table and takes a seat right next to Mathew. We wait in silence, eyeing each other down; Mathew trying to look comforting while Nichelle looks annoyed.

Finally, the door opens and a man enters with Greyson and Aiden to the side of him. They both look confused, looking around, but show no signs of being harmed. Aiden doesn't have his hood on and his hands are out, making me wonder if they came from inside the building or if darkness has arrived

"Please, have a seat," Mathew says, gesturing at the table.

Aiden's eyes land on me and he rushes over to sit beside me while Greyson walks to the other side of the table and takes a seat opposite of Mathew.

"Where's Maci?" I ask Aiden.

"They patched her up and she's resting in a room," he answers, staring Mathew down with a cold, hard glare. "Who's the old guy?"

Before I can explain, Mathew clears his throat. "First, I want to apologize to each of you for the way we welcomed you. You need to understand that it was only done to protect the people of this town. We needed to be positive that none of you had been infected by the virus." He pauses and directs his attention at Aiden. "Or that any of you would be a danger to us."

"If you thought we would be dangerous, why did you bring us here?" I interrupt, putting my arms on the table, reminding them that I still have the knife.

Mathew's pale eyes glance at the knife then at me. "I didn't expect you to arrive with others. It surprised me. Also, when we saw the wounds and blood on Maci, we needed to make sure she wasn't bitten; that none of you were."

I place my knife on the table and fold my arms. "I can understand that. We all want to protect those we belong to."

He nods in agreement. "Exactly." A bead of sweat drips down from his forehead and he wipes it on his sleeve. I remember that Nichelle told me earlier that Mathew had been bitten. I wonder if he is changing, if he is putting his people at risk right now.

"Nichelle told me you were bitten," I say. "Yet you haven't changed. How is that possible?"

"That isn't the reason I brought you here," he replies, looking pale and worn out. "When I worked with the doctors at the colony, we were experimenting with our medications on animals. It was difficult to see what kind of results we were getting. So Gabrielle and Monarch began stealing children for our experiments. They rationalized their antics by telling themselves they would only steal children who had been neglected or abused in their homes."

Aiden's eyes flicker with rage. "That's bull. Sylas and I were never neglected or abused by our parents."

Michelle glances over at him, the expression on his face seems sad. "I'm not sure how come the two of you were chosen, but after they stole you, they had to slow down with the amount of children that they were stealing. Your parents did a massive search trying to find you. Everyone at the colony worried we'd all be found and then locked away. But after a period of time they gave up the search."

Aiden jumps up, toppling his chair over. "Stop lying."

Nichelle instantly jumps up in front of Mathew, putting herself between Aiden and him. "Watch it. I'm not afraid to take you out."

Aiden laughs sardonically, throwing his head back. "Like you could."

She glares at him, her voice dropping low with a warning, "Want to find out?"

Aiden laughs again, but it fizzles out and his angry gaze focuses on Mathew. "So you knew about everything? You were a part of it?" he asks Mathew. "How can you stand to live with yourself after the torture you put all of us through?" He's shaking from head to toe and I can tell he's about to do something based on his anger.

I gently place my hand on Aiden's arm. He glances at it as I pull him back down in his chair. "Easy, okay? Let's hear what he has to say."

Mathew's looks remorseful and Nichelle also sits back down. "When I found out how bad things were," he explains, "the horrible experiments, the torture that were being conducted, I didn't stay. I left the colony and came here. But it was already too late to stop the cycle of what was happening. All I could do was try to prepare myself and as many others as possible, for what was going to be inevitable."

"Cedrix told me that the world is this way because of greed," I say. "Can you tell us what happened? How the world became this way; how the vampires came into existence?"

He looks surprised. "You know Cedrix?" he asks and I nod in response. "He's one of the few doctors that tried to put an end to the madness before it became worse."

"I knew him," I tell him. "We all did... but he's not alive anymore."

Mathew's eyes fill with anguish and he lets out a deep sigh as he looks down at his hands. "I'm sad to say that I'm not surprised. Death is more common than life anymore." He returns his eyes to me and they're watery, something I don't understand. "And he was right when he told you that it was greed that started this. He knew exactly how it all started; we all did because we were all part of it. We are all responsible." He takes a trembling breath. "And the reason the vampires came into existence was all because of one little girl named Kayla."

My jaw drops. I'm shocked, stunned and a little pissed off, amongst other things. Everyone looks in my direction, waiting for me to say something or hurt them.

102

I shake my head, my hands starting to tremble. "You're lying."

"Kayla, please calm down," Mathew says. "I'm not saying you're responsible. The doctors kept trying different injections on all the children. Usually they would end up dying or worse, turn into something that was half-dead, half-alive. However, when the injected you, it was as if your body became stronger and adapted to each serum they tried. Monarch decided to turn you into a perfect soldier. He didn't allow you to make any connections with children. There was a day in the lab when he thought everything was perfect and he tricked you into biting someone."

I can remember sinking my teeth into someone very well. "Gabrielle," I say quietly.

"Yes, and that day started the change," he explains. "Gabrielle immediately knew that he was changing into something; something stronger and more powerful than he had ever imagined. The rest of the doctors became excited and envious; they wanted to experience the same thing. So they injected themselves with the virus. The shot was called the fountain of youth; it would provide eternal life to those who took it. By that time, I'd left the colony, but from what

I understand, the virus was marketed to the elite within the next few weeks. These elite groups of people became known as the Highers."

"But something went wrong with the virus?" Aiden asks, pushing up the sleeves of his jacket.

Mathew nods, reclining in his chair. "It wasn't too long after that when the Highers developed a thirst for blood and started feeding off humans. In addition, there was something about the Highers' bite that caused people to forget that they'd been bit. But the humans could only endure so many bites from the Highers before something caused them to become infected with a terrible virus. A virus that turned them into what we now call vampires. As you know, a vampire's bite is deadly and immediately infects their victim, causing their disease to spread and turn their victim."

Everything makes sense but I still don't understand something. I remember seeing the Highers feeding off the vampires.

"But why did I see the Highers feeding on the vampires?" I question him.

"Human blood no longer fulfills them. And there's something different with the composition of the vampire blood that allows the Highers to maintain their looks and strength. There's a rumor going around that the Highers are becoming immune to the effects of the vampires' blood and they need to come up with a different solution or their race may end."

It's all starting to make perfect sense. The bite of Gabrielle. The Highers feeding on the vampires, but why does it feel like something's missing?

"When I was captured by Monarch and Gabrielle, I was told me they needed me alive to save their race," I tell him. "Why?"

"I'm not sure… it does make sense, though, since the vampire's blood is beginning to lose its effectiveness for them." He pauses. "They're probably trying to go back to the original source again. Start over and find another cure. They will need you to do that." He clasps his hands together in front of him, contemplating something. "Whatever happens, we must make sure they don't capture you again. We can't risk them finding a cure if they are beginning to weaken."

I note Mathew's pale eyes again. "You never did explain to me why you look like a Higher," I point out with wariness.

"Before I left the colony, I injected myself with one of the viruses that I believed to be a cure from the bite of a vampire. It had no effect on me until I was bitten a few weeks ago." He spreads his hands out to the side of him. "This is what has happened since then."

Aiden leans forward in his chair, his leg pushing against mine from under the table. I wonder if he's doing it on purpose or if he even knows he is. "So, you are trying to tell us that you were bitten by a vampire weeks ago and are still alive? Because I find all of this hard to believe."

Nichelle shoots Aiden a harsh look, her jaw tightening. "It's true. We had some vampires break through our barricades. We lost many of our people." She looks at Mathew with pride. "Mathew tried to defend the town, but was bitten on the leg."

He returns her grin and she directs her attention back to Aiden, her eyes darkening. "A few weeks have passed and here he stands, not infected at all."

Mathew looks at her sadly. "I haven't turned yet, but I can feel it coming. It's only a matter of time."

"What do you mean it's only a matter of time? How can you tell?" Greyson asks curiously. He's been so quiet through all this, I almost forgot that he was here.

106

Mathew seems uncomfortable with his question and shifts in his chair, moving forward then deciding to lean back again, as though he can't figure out what to do with himself. "I started hallucinating that my skin was falling off. I've actually had to check in the mirror several times to make sure it's not really happening."

Aiden raises his eyebrows at me, bumps my knee from under the table and then whispers, "Do you really believe him?"

I'm not sure. I'm not sure of anything anymore.

"Are you sure that you're not putting anyone at risk; that you're not changing?" I ask Mathew.

"Mathew wouldn't put anybody at risk," Nichelle snaps. "He's always been the one who tries to help others."

Mathew puts his hand on Nichelle's and gives her an affectionate look. "Nichelle's right. If I think that I'm becoming dangerous to anyone, I'll make sure the right thing is done."

Greyson looks at Mathew with disappointment. "So your change has only been delayed. Does that mean that there's no cure?" He frowns.

Mathew takes a folded piece of paper out of his pocket then he puts it onto the table and smoothes out the wrinkles. There's something written on it, but since I can't read. I don't know what it says.

"Not too long ago a man came in search of me," he says. "He claimed to be sent here by Monarch, and he told me that Monarch wasn't sure if I was still alive, but if I was, he was to deliver this paper to me. From what I remember of Monarch's handwriting, I'm pretty sure the man wasn't lying and Monarch did write this." He taps his finger on the paper.

"What does it say?" I ask, glancing at Aiden, wondering if he can read it.

"Apparently, Monarch had a change of heart and wanted to reverse the damage that he caused," Mathew explains. "He finally discovered a cure and wrote it down. He was afraid that he'd be caught, so he hid the information in his office at the colony."

I know what papers he's talking about. They are the ones that Sylas and I found earlier. I'm not sure why Monarch would tell Mathew about them when he was so careful to make sure that he removed all my memories and put them into Aiden, so that his plans to save the world would stay hidden.

"Why would he tell you about them?" I ask Mathew with caution.

"He told me about everything in this letter... his plans for an army of Day Takers and how you're the only Day Walker. He wanted a backup plan to make sure that there was someone else that knew about the cure. I guess, because I wasn't happy when the virus was created, he assumed that I'd want to make sure a cure was found."

"So what we need are those papers that are hidden?" Aiden asks, raking his fingers through his hair, leaving it sticking up everywhere. "If they are still even there."

"They're there," I tell them. They all look at me inquisitively, waiting for me to explain further.

"How do you know?" Nichelle asks skeptically, glancing at the knife in front of me.

"Because I've already found them," I tell them, putting my hand over the knife, ready to use it if needed.

"You have them?" Mathew asks, his eyes lighting up.

I shake my head. "I *had* them. But when Sylas and I were attacked, I dropped them."

"Do you think that Gabrielle has them?" Aiden asks, frowning.

I bite my lip, deliberating. "I don't think so. There were other papers scattered all over the room to begin with, so I'm pretty sure that no one even noticed when I dropped them, but then again, I can't be one-hundred percent sure." *I can't be one-hundred percent sure of anything.*

"Then we should go get them," Nichelle says with way too much enthusiasm. "If we hurry, maybe we can make the cure before..." She trails off as she glances over at Mathew.

She's right. We should go get the papers and bring them back. Mathew is one of the original doctors. He has a better chance of understanding what Monarch wrote down then any of us. He may be able to make the cure. Besides, even though I don't want to admit it, I am hoping that if we go back there's a chance that I can find Sylas. I hate that I'm getting my hopes up, though, when deep down I know it's never going to happen. *Sylas is gone.*

"You're right," I say to Nichelle, collecting my knife from the table. "*We* do need to go get them, but *you* need to stay here."

"I'm perfectly capable of taking care of myself," she says harshly. "Besides, you may need my help."

"Nichelle, Kayla's right," Mathew interrupts, placing his hand over hers again. "You need to stay here. The vampires are becoming more aggressive and it is becoming more difficult to keep them out of town. We need your help here. Kayla and Aiden are more than capable of doing this by themselves. They just need to be careful not to run into any Highers."

Greyson looks at both Aiden and I. "What about me and Maci? What should we do?"

"Is it all right if they stay with you?" I ask Mathew, hoping upon hope that I'm not making a mistake. That he's trustworthy and won't hurt them

He nods and relief washes over me because, even though I don't want to say it aloud, I don't want to have to take them with us. They'll only slow us down.

"You have to promise me that you'll let nothing happen to Maci," I tell Mathew with a warning in my tone.

He nods. "I will make sure nothing happens to her. I promise," he says truthfully.

I turn to Aiden who is watching me with curiosity. Before I can even open my mouth to ask him if he wants to go, he says, "When are we leaving?"

I almost want to tell him to stay behind, but at the same time, if something happened to me, it'll be good if he's there to step in and finish the job; to save the world. It might be getting dark and the vampires will be roaming, yet for Aiden and I, that doesn't matter. *So weird.*

"Now," I say, the strangeness of the situation even more evident.

He stands up and waits for me by the door with his hands stuffed in his pockets.

I get to my feet. "Give us two days," I tell Mathew. "That should give us enough time to get there and back."

He nods and then I motion for Greyson to come over to me. Nichelle and Mathew give me a strange look, but don't say anything as he winds around the table and huddles up with me.

"If anything weird happens at all," I tell him in a low voice, "get Maci out of here."

He squirms uneasily, scratching at the back of his neck. "Where should I go?"

"To the caves back up on the hill. And hide out there until Aiden or I return."

He reluctantly nods and then Aiden and I open the door to head out, unsure of how dangerous it is, though I am certain that there will be dangers. Not with the vampires, but with the abominations; the unknown. Plus, we're walking into the Highers' territory.

"Kayla, Aiden, please be careful," Mathew calls out as I'm shutting the door. "We need you to return; we need those papers."

I nod and then we leave, walking down a hall, and moments later, we're outside. The sky is dark, the air chilly, and the vampires' cries greet us from the distance; however, we don't have to be afraid.

The town has a wall built around it made from old vehicles and scraps of metal. Guards are posted on top of the barricade with knives, ready to kill anything that threatens to try to break through. Aiden and I climb on top of one of the barricades so we can jump over to the other side. There are two guards posted there, one short and round, the other tall and sturdy. The tall one steps in front of me as I attempt to hoist myself over a smashed-in car and to the other side.

113

"What do you think you are doing?" He walks up to me, his boots crunching against the dirt and rocks and he almost steps on my fingers. "You can't leave town now. It's getting dark."

"Your rules don't apply to us," I tell him as I push myself on top. Rules. I hate rules.

"Leave them alone, Earl," the other one says, moving his knife to his other hand as he stares out at the opposite direction from us. "They're part freak. Can't you tell?" They both laugh at us.

Aiden jumps back over onto the car, heading towards them, fist clenched and raised. I quickly stand up and latch onto his arm, pulling him towards me as I back to the edge of the barricade. I keep backing up until we reach the edge then I tug him with me as I hop down to the other side, landing with a soft thud in the dirt.

"Let me go." He jerks his arm away from me and starts back towards the wall where the guards look down at us, still laughing under their breath.

"It's not worth it, Aiden." I grab the collar of his jacket and drag him backward then I take his hand and start to walk away out into the hills and desert.

"Yes, it is." He grins as he looks down at our hands that are clasped together.

I shake my head, wanting to smack him. "You know that's not what I meant."

I try to let go of his hand, but he tightens his grip. "Can't we just enjoy it for a second?" he asks as I wind downward into a group of towering rocks.

I resist the urge to pull my hand away and try to find the enjoyment he suggests, wondering if I can get there, but I can't. Honestly, I don't really feel anything at all, except the slight chilliness of his skin. My mind wanders back to Sylas and the kiss we shared before Gabrielle captured us. A spark of sadness hits me as I think of what he has turned into. How he no longer exists and has become a monster, that he might have been one of those things running around on the street.

"You look sad... what are you thinking about?" Aiden asks, his eyes sweeping the path in front of us—the rocks, the bushes—his body tensing with every vampire cry, as if he's still not used to being able to walk with them.

"Nothing important," I mutter. "I just hope we're not too late to find the papers," I lie. My thoughts are still firmly planted on Sylas and the kiss. I can almost visualize him changing into some unknown horror of a monster and I simply left him. What the hell? Why did I do that? Why am I so worried about it now? Why do I feel so... so guilty?

"You know Kayla, we don't need to go back to the colony; we don't have to get the papers and take them back," he says, tugging on my arm and moving me to the side as a snake slithers across the ground in front of us.

I gape at him, slamming to a stop. "Are you being serious right now? Because getting those papers is pretty much the only hope for humanity."

"Who says humanity is worth saving? Maybe this," he points at himself and me, "is what is really supposed to happen to the world. Maybe we *are* perfection," he says smugly and starts walking again, pulling me with him.

I jerk my hand from his. "What the hell's happened to you? You've changed and I don't think I like it."

He shrugs, stepping to the side, putting distance between us. "I've changed into something better." I glare at him and he smiles. "Look at us, Kayla, the vampires won't bite us. We are fast. We are strong. When we are hurt we heal almost instantly. I haven't seen you drink any blood and I know that I don't have the thirst for it. We are basically invincible. Isn't this better than being a weak human and having to worry about surviving every day? It's as if we are *perfect*."

I'm about to tell him that he's a complete jerk and lost his mind that sounds just like the Highers but I'm interrupted by a hoard of vampires that are blocking the trail in front of us. They're spread out across the path and between the rocks and they viciously snarl and snap their teeth at us; some stepping forward and some moving back like a rippling wave.

Aiden smirks at them and then at me, giving me the most arrogant look, before he takes off and charges headfirst towards the group, bringing his knife out as he charges. He jumps into the air right before he reaches the line of them and kicks his feet out in front of him, knocking down the front ones before he lands in a crouch. Quickly springing up, he slashes flesh and stabs them in the heart, moving at a speed my eyes can barely detect; I almost start to worry that he's faster than me. The vampires explode into dust one by one while any that are left take a whiff of the air and start to retreat back into the shadows and down into the flat area of the land, letting out shriek after shriek.

Aiden strolls towards me gloating. "See what I mean." He tucks his knife into his pocket and brushes dust off his hands. "This is much better. We kill them instead of them killing us. We're the only ones that can control them."

He is completely different than he was before he changed. When I changed, I felt better, stronger, but I didn't lose my sense of compassion for the human race. Not like Aiden seems to have done.

He's right. We're the only ones that can control them, but it still doesn't mean that this is what the world comes to. That we're the future of humanity. There's still so much we can do. We can still save the world.

Flashing me a grin, Aiden turns and strides off towards the hill like he's proving he's faster than me. I watch him as he makes his way up the hill while I trudge behind him, wondering if he's lost all of the humanity inside of him.

If the Aiden I first met is completely gone. If he is—it will be completely up to me to bring those papers back.

Chapter 13

We hike the rest of the night, being quiet and keeping a bit of space between us. A few vampires appear in front of us occasionally, but Aiden is quick to make sure that they know who we are and what they are dealing with by running at them with his knife and baring his fangs. When he's within a few steps of them, they backtrack and disappear behind the rocks, howling at one another and snapping their fangs, starving, but knowing they can't feed on us.

Eventually, the cave that we hid in earlier comes into view just as daylight is getting ready to kiss the land, trickling drops of light breaking through the foggy sky. Aiden hurriedly veers towards the entrance and I wonder what the hell he's doing.

"Where are you going?" I call out as I keep walking straight.

He turns around at the edge of a boulder and raises his arms above his head, showing me his torn sleeves and the massive amount of tears throughout the fabric. "I guess I got a little carried away," he says, seeming proud. "I'll have to hide out until the sun goes down."

Part of me thinks he did it on purpose. Part of me wants to leave him. Part of me wants to knock him out.

Shaking my head, I change directions and head towards the cave. Aiden rushes inside just as the sun glimmers over the horizon. I stand outside deliberating on whether to keep going or wait, since I'm not sure if he's even going to help me or not then. I ultimately settle on waiting, more because I worry what he'll do if I leave him behind. Go back to the colony maybe and do something bad? At this point, I wouldn't put it past him. Still, I find myself wishing I had some silver or something to knock him out with... although I'm not sure if it'd work since Aiden seems a lot different from a Day Taker.

I sit down outside on a rock with my knife in my hand, my elbow propped on my knee and my chin resting on my hand. I watch as the sky turns grey, lost in my thoughts.

"We can't let the Highers find out about your perfection," Monarch tells me as he rummages through his medicine cupboards. *"If they do, then everything we've done to save the world will become pointless."*

"But what about Aiden? What if they find out about him?" I ask as I climb up on an empty hospital bed. "Won't he put everything at risk, too?"

Monarch shakes his head as he looks at me. "I've told you that even though Aiden's the only other one like you, he's broken."

"Broken how?" I look down at my arm as he places a needle full of black fluid into my skin.

"Kayla, we've talked about you asking too many questions. You need to stop. Concentrate on everything you've been trained to do." He pushes the needle deeper into my skin, injecting more dark liquid into my vein.

"But…" Everything goes blurry and I collapse onto the bed as I fade into unconsciousness.

"Kayla, are you going to sit out there all day?" Aiden's voice brings me back to reality.

I sigh and glance over at the entrance of the cave. Aiden is standing near the edge of the shadows with his hood down, watching me with a puzzled look, as if he doesn't understand why I won't go in there with him. I climb off the rock and hop down to the flat space in front of the cave, staying in the sunlight. "Did you really mean everything you said last night? About it being better for humans to change into the same breed as we are?"

Aiden looks at me intensely, leaning forward just the slightest bit. "Kayla, please, just let it go."

I back away from him, putting more and more space between us. "You're not trying to manipulate my thoughts again, are you? Because you know it doesn't work on me."

He holds his hands out in front of him. "Relax. I wasn't trying to do anything to you. I was simply trying to figure you out. Why can't you see that what we are is better?"

"What happened to the Aiden that thought that becoming a Day Taker was the wrong choice? The Aiden who cared about people?" I ask him, storming back towards him.

"That Aiden was naive and stupid," he says, inching to the edge of the line where the shadows meet the daylight. "He didn't understand what it was like to be fearless, strong, perfect." He tries to grab me, but I'm too fast, jumping out of his reach.

I glare at him and narrow my eyes as I back towards the rocks again, deciding what to do. Walk away? Stay?

Hurt him? "If you're so perfect, then how come you are stuck there in the shadows?" I raise my eyebrows at him, challenging him, then tip my chin back and look up at the grey sky. "You're flawed and your inability to go in the daylight isn't what I'm talking about. You're cold and uncaring. I'd much rather have the human Aiden than what you have become." I turn my back on him and walk away.

Aiden growls, furious, and bursts out of the cave into the light, running straight at me. Without thinking, I spin around to shove him back, but it is too late. Sun blankets him as he stumbles back, still out of the shade of the cave. There's a moment where he doesn't realize what's going on then he sees my terrified expression and his gaze drifts down at his hands. Time seems to slow down, yet the more time that slips by, the more aware we both become that nothing is happening. He doesn't burst into dust as the sun touches his face, his hands, his arms. Aiden's a Day Taker. Monarch told me that Aiden was broken, but apparently his flaw is not the sun.

A grin spreads across Aiden's face as he holds his hands up to the sky. "See, we *are* perfect."

I roll my eyes, resisting the urge to shove him to the ground.

He drops his hands back to his side and walks over next to me, placing his hands on my shoulders. "You know I would never hurt you, right?"

"I know you *can't* hurt me," I say then let out a breath of frustration. "Aiden, I care for you and everything; I don't want you to become something different just because you suddenly feel powerful."

His expression falls, but it quickly vanishes. "You care for me, yet you don't love me?"

"I don't love anyone," I say, but for some reason it feels like a lie.

"That's not true. You love Sylas." He waits for me to deny it.

I open my mouth, planning on denying, but for some reason, the words won't leave me.

"Don't worry," he says, pretending to be nonchalant about it when really I can tell he's hurt. "I'll always be here for you. Especially now that Sylas is gone." Then his mood shifts, and suddenly, he's back to being as cheerful as can be; a bounce in his walk as he breezes by me towards the path. "Well, since daylight isn't a problem, how about we go get those papers?"

I can feel lies radiating from him, although I can't figure out what they are or where they're coming from. He's so moody and I know I'm going to have to be on my guard. Either that or knock him out and leave him somewhere.

As I follow behind him beneath the faint flow of the sun, Monarch's words keep echoing through my head. *He's the only other one like you, but he's broken. Broken.*

I'm beginning to think that Monarch meant he is broken in the head. I wonder if he'll ever be able to be fixed; go back to being the same Aiden he used to be. The one that cared for others. The one that I cared about, in a way. Because right now, I don't care about him, and if he tries to put humans or me at risk, I'll stop him no matter what it takes.

Chapter 14

It's a long journey and exhausting, but only because Aiden makes it that way by being happy one minute and rude the next. His mood swings are tiring. Finally, though, we're walking across the park where Sylas, Aiden and I once played when we were smaller. The place where Sylas gave me a flower on my birthday... one of my rare, good memories, well, at least the beginning of it anyway.

"Is something amusing?" Aiden asks, watching me intently.

I realize I'm smiling and quickly erase it as I focus on the building across from the park where the papers were left behind. He practically burns a hole in my head, trying to decipher what I'm really thinking about, but I ignore him and speed up, leaving him a trailing behind me.

As we reach the building, I veer to the right and head towards the doorway that's covered with torn plastic, which I cut open the last time I was here. I carefully push the plastic aside and peek into the building. It looks vacant, so I cautiously duck through the hole, glancing around at the empty space, the plastic above. Nothing else seems to be around.

I motion for Aiden to follow me and he ducks through the plastic, looking around the empty room curiously. "So where are the papers that we need?" he asks, turning in a circle, looking at the walls and the ceiling.

I nod, holding my finger up to my lips. "Shhh… We don't want to get caught and be locked up," I hiss.

He shrugs my comments off and begins to wander around the room, like he doesn't care if we get caught. I dash across the room towards the hall and turn down it in the direction of where I dropped the papers; where I last kissed Sylas.

When I reach the room I cautiously peer around the corner to make sure it is empty. I then step inside quietly. I the papers still scattered over the floor with droplets of dried blood on them I rush over towards it,

I bend down quickly to collect them as they flap in a gentle breeze blowing from somewhere inside of the building. I have a few papers in my hand when I am startled by a noise through the doorway next to me. The doorway that leads into the cell area I was locked in. I slide my knife out of my pocket, setting the papers down on the ground before I make my way towards the noise. I step through the doorway keeping my guard up, as I walk down between the glass cages. Peering in each of them as I walk by, secretly hoping that Sylas will be inside one of them and that's who made the noise that I heard.

"You know that he is gone, right?" Aiden's voice rises up behind me. I whirl around in surprise, ready to fight. He's standing in the doorway staring at me looking slightly upset. "But here you are. Still hoping that somehow Sylas will be inside one of these cages."

"I thought I heard a noise." I give him a dirty look.

Choosing to ignore him, I check the rest of the cages, but of course they're all empty. When I turn back around, Aiden's no longer standing in the doorway and I quicken my pace until I reach the end of the cells. I stop to pick papers, and I can't help but glance at the spot on the floor where Sylas and I kissed, memories hitting my mind like pinpricks. I tear my gaze away before it becomes too much then bend over to scoop the papers up from the floor. I stack them in my arms and head towards the door when Aiden steps in front of me, putting his arms on the doorway like a barricade.

"You're really going to do it, aren't you? Can't you see that you're wrong? We need to change the world. Make the rest of the world like us…" He pauses and I see a threatening glint in his eyes that puts me on high alert. "Well, at least the people in the world that we feel are worthy to be like us."

"Move out of my way, Aiden," I say in a calm, yet firm voice. "This isn't the place or time to fight about this." I shove him, but he doesn't budge.

"I can't let you do it. I won't let you." His fangs slide out and he bares them at me.

Tucking the papers under my arm, I aim the knife at him. "Now get out of my way, or I'll make you get out of my way.

He laughs, however the amusement quickly leaves his face as a misshapen form emerges from the room to the side of us. My body tenses as I hear the growl. I slowly turn, pointing my knife at it, bending my knees, ready to plunge into the monster. Another one appears just behind Aiden, snarling as it creeps towards us on all fours.

I put the papers down, moving slowly—keeping my eyes fixed on the monster to the side of me. I take a deep breath and then without warning, I dash over to it. It nips at me as I reach its front and I skitter to the side, going around. Blood drips out of its mouth as it turns with me, following my movements as I shuffle towards the wall.

Its crooked legs bring it closer to me as I back towards the wall, searching for a way out. When it's within reach, I bring my foot up and slam the tip of my toe into its mouth. Blood splatters on the ground as it lets out a shrill howl then barrels at me. I swing my knife down right as it's about to take a bite of my leg. The blade enters its spongy body and it cries out as I plunge the knife deeper. Blood gushes out as I wrench the knife out and flip back as the monster lurches towards me. I spin and sink the knife inside of its chest, slashing open the skin. It howls again, so loudly I want to cover my ears, then it flops down on its side, blood pooling around it.

It continues to snap its teeth at me for a moment until its head falls to its side as its body goes limp. For a second I just stare at it, wondering if it could have been Sylas, which only hurts to think about.

Panting, I spin around just in time to see Aiden finish off the other beast, slamming his knife deep into the monster's chest. Blood spurts out of the wound as he removes the knife and backs up. The monster lets out a furious cry and then drops to the floor like a bag of bricks. I wipe the blade of my knife over my jeans, pick the papers up, then without saying anything to Aiden, I hurry to the plastic and duck outside.

I can hear Aiden's footsteps as he rapidly catches up with me and grabs my arm. I shrug him off and continue walking.

"Kayla, we need to talk," he demands, striding alongside of me.

I turn the corner and stride towards the park, hugging the papers tightly to my chest. When he grabs my shoulder again, I whirl around and push him back, ready to get out of here, save the world and forget. Forget about everything. The choices I've made, the things...

I stop walking as I reach the spot where the land opens up. There are dozens of abominations standing in front of us, down on all fours, drooling on the ground as they look at us with hunger in their eyes.

"Let's take them," Aiden says, stepping forward with a pleased look on his face.

I grab his arm and pull him back. "No way. There's too many of them."

He looks torn, glancing back and forth between them and me. He surprises me, though, when he nods and we spin around together to start running back in the direction we came from.

I think that Aiden is following me until I throw a glance over my shoulder and realize he's running in a different direction, heading towards a few dead trees. As he yells at the beasts and makes a lot of noise, I wonder what he's doing, but then I realize he's trying to get them away from me. I'm not sure how that makes me feel. I had pretty much made up my mind that Aiden was not good anymore.

His plan almost works and most of the monsters chase after him, tearing up the ground with their claws, but a few of them look at me with their hungry eyes and run after me. I pump my legs faster, barreling back towards the building, knowing I've outrun them before and I can do it again.

All but one of them starts to fall behind and I begin to relax until one seems to be gaining on me. It's nipping at my heels, making loud growls, ripping up pieces of the ground with his force. I feel myself reaching maximum speed and I don't know what to do because it seems to be getting closer. I spot a pile of rusty cars just in front of me. Not knowing what else to do, I quickly dive to the side of them and squeeze in between a metal gap. I barely get my legs inside as it tries to take a bite, barely missing my skin. As I shimmy farther into the pile of cars, I draw out my knife. It puts its eyes up to the gap and watches me, letting out a low growl. I keep going until I reach the end of the gap and, when I turn around, the monster is gone.

I tentatively stick my head out of the hole and glance around. It is silent, but the quietness makes me uneasy. I lie there for a little bit longer, clutching onto the papers and my knife.

Finally, after the quietness lingers for a while, I duck my head out and fall to the ground, rolling out. I jump to my feet and brush the dirt off me letting out a breath of relief. The sound of a deep growl from behind me makes my hairs stand on end.

I turn around slowly and meet the eyes of a beast that is much larger than the rest of the heard, its flesh rotting off of it and falling to the ground. I start to bring my knife around, but it dips its head towards me. Its teeth piercing through my pants leg to my flesh, sinking deep into my muscles.

My knife falls to the ground as my legs give out on me and I fall. The last thing I see is the monster watching me. I know that soon I'll become one of them.

Chapter 15

Everything hurts. Throbs. I don't know where I am.

What happened? What's going on? I don't know anything.

Then my mind starts to focus and I let out a small cry, almost by instinct. Oh God. I start to remember. The feeling of teeth sinking into flesh. Am… am I becoming one of them?

My eyelids flutter open. I'm no longer in the park, but in a dark room, lying on my back on top of some sort of blanket that is spread out on the hard stone floor. *How did I get here? How long have I been unconscious? Am I changing now? Or am I immune like with the vampires?*

I raise my arms up in front of me and check them over then slowly sit up and inspect my legs. Besides the tear in my jeans and the teeth gashes on my skin, I show no signs of turning into an abomination. The bite marks on my leg is tender, aching, and I blood is still trickling out of it. *They haven't healed yet. Not a good sign.*

In the corner of the room is a stack of crates, and on top of it is my knife and the papers I was carrying. I gradually get to me feet, scanning the room as I carefully make my way over to it.

I need to get out of here, find Aiden in case I do end up changing and make sure he understands that he needs to kill me before I do, and get the papers back to Mathew. Although, if his attitude is the same, I have no idea how I'm going to get him to agree with me and *if* I can even trust him.

When I reach the crate, I crouch down to gather my things, my muscles aching in protest. I get the knife in my hand when I notice movement from the other side. I quickly stand back up taking a step back and listen for the sound of a heartbeat, hoping that I hear one. Hoping that what lies behind the crate is human. But the only noise that I can hear is the sound of labored breathing and I'm not sure what it belongs to.

Moving vigilantly around the crate with my knife in my hand, I peer down at the other side. The first thing that comes into view is a hand, but it's not a human hand. It's starting to rot, flesh peeling away and it looks like it belongs to someone who is in the process of turning.

I continue around to the other side of the crate and the hand rapidly pulls out of my sight as someone scurries farther behind it.

"Back off, Kayla. It is not safe... I'm not safe." The voice is rough and scratchy.

"Aiden?"

There's no response, but it has to be him. I glance down at my arms, turning them over, and my skin still as pale and smooth. It doesn't make any sense. I'm not changing yet, but he is. Why? I thought we were the same.

I look around at the unfamiliar room again. Why did he bring me here instead of taking me out of the colony where we'd be safer? Or to the desert?

"Did you bring me here?" I ask, stepping around the crate trying to get closer. "Did you save me from that monster?"

I take a few more steps towards him, listening to his labored breathing. His arms come into view, his flesh is strange looking, like it's trying to melt. "Maybe if we hurry we can go back to the town and get help."

"I can't," he croaks. "I can't go anywhere just yet."

"We have to," I say, swallowing hard, not sure if I want to take the last few steps to see him changing. "If you're changing... if we both change... we have to make sure the papers get back to the colony."

"No," he says almost sharply.

Frustrated, I turn for the door, ready to leave, knowing that I might be running out of time... I might have to run the entire way there.

As I'm getting ready to exit, the memory of Sylas replays in my mind. I remember him begging me not to let him turn; pleading with me to end him before he changed. Guilt spreads through me and I pause in front of the door. I can't just leave him here like this, let him change into one of those horrible creatures, even though he's done things I don't like—said terrible things, he still deserves not to turn into a monster.

I set the papers down again and turn around. I slowly walk back towards the crate, worried about what I'll say, what he'll say to me with what I'm about to do. Then the crates abruptly shift slowly and he pushes himself to his feet. He doesn't have a shirt on and his dark hair is matted to the back of his head. He is standing tall with his back towards me, like he knows what I'm about to do.

I carefully walk up behind him, wondering if he knows, if he understands. I almost change my mind—I am not sure if I can do it. I am not sure if I can kill him.

However, I swallow my feelings as I take in the sight of his skin that hangs loosely from his body with open wounds which are bleeding.

Elevating the knife above my head, I aim it at his back, ready to plunge it deep inside him, end him and help his suffering. But before I can move he spins around, his dark eyes instantly focusing on the knife. Before I can change my mind, I quickly thrust the knife towards him.

His eyes widen, his arm snaps out and he grabs hold of my wrist, stopping the knife just a fraction before it clips his skin.

"Kayla, stop." He tightly grips my hand and I struggle, trying to break free, twisting my arm. "Kayla, look at me."

I'm not sure what registers first; his command, the change in his voice, or the sudden feeling of calmness that fills me. I stop fighting and look up at him, meeting his gaze and gasp as he lets me go. My hand falls to my side and the knife slips from my fingers, landing on the floor with a clink. It can't be.

Yet the more I look at him, the more I know it's true. The cold, dark eyes that are looking back at me don't belong to Aiden, they belong to Sylas.

Chapter 16

For a while, neither of us can speak and it is quiet. Maybe Sylas is just waiting for me to say something, but it seems like I've lost my voice. He looks so different, still him—black hair, eyes like charcoal, a slight cocky expression—but beneath it is pain. Pain from his flesh rotting? Pain from changing? Or is it because I left him to change?

"Aren't you going to say anything?" he finally asks, stretching out his long legs.

Say what? I'm too speechless to speak. "Why... I mean how can you be still changing? When I saw you last, you were already turning. And that was a while ago."

He shrugs nonchalantly but his eyes are full of emotion, though I can't tell exactly what. "I did turn. I turned into one of those horrible monsters. It was like being stuck in a bad dream..." His forehead creases in puzzlement as his head cocks to the side. "Until I bit you."

"What? You changed and then you changed back?" I ask, shocked, wanting to pick up my knife. Thinking it may help this lost, helpless feeling inside me; one I've never felt before. "I don't understand, Sylas. Aren't the effects of the bite permanent?"

He sighs tiredly then steps backward to the crate and hoists himself up on top, his arms wobbling as he does it. He sits on it with his bare feet hanging over it. "Oh, the effects were permanent. Well, at least they were supposed to be. But when I bit you, I could feel something in me start to change. The instant my teeth sunk into your skin, something ignited inside me and I knew I had to stop hurting you, like it was an instinct."

"So, you bit me?"

He shrugs again, but there's a hungry look in his eye that makes my skin feel hot. "Well, do you really blame me?"

I try my best to shake it off, but the fact that he's sitting here, not hurt and *almost* not an abomination, is making it hard not to want to do anything except hug him and tell him that I'm sorry for leaving him. "So do you think my bite cured you?"

"Maybe… Monarch did make you special after all, but then again we know little about the abominations," he says with almost a thoughtful expression as he assesses me.

"The one he wanted to be perfect." He pauses, glancing down at his own skin, amazed at the sight of it healing.

I take a step closer to him and touch his arm. I'm not even sure why I do it other than I feel this need to touch him, to feel that he's real, so I trace my fingers over one of his open wounds. The bleeding is now barely noticeable as his skin continues to heal itself.

"This is amazing." I say. "You're really changing back."

"Yeah, it is."

I look up and meet his eyes. The hunger is there again and instead of wanting to run away from him, I want to get closer to him, like I did when I thought he was dying. I place my hand on his cheek. His skin feels cold and sort of rough, almost unnatural, yet I don't pull back.

I'm not even sure at what the point of my touching him is, but before I can figure it out, he grabs my hand and jerks me into him, eliminating any space left between our bodies. He slams his lips against mine and kisses me passionately, his hands wandering down my back as he presses me closer to him. He tastes strange, like rust, yet at the same time, he tastes good, and I realize how much I've worried about him while we've been apart.

What does that mean? About my feelings towards him? Something... I can feel it... this is so much different than with Aiden... so much more... sweltering and hard to breathe.

He pulls back abruptly, his lips a little swollen, giving me barely any time to react as I stumble back from the disconnection. "I shouldn't have done that," he says.

"Why?" I frown because it doesn't sound like something he'd say at all.

"Because..." He drags his fingers through his hair roughly, looking stressed out and Sylas never looks stressed. "It may not be safe; *I* may not be safe. I mean, we know nothing about this process... changing back." His gaze encounters mine. "What if I hurt you or infect you?"

I'm not sure how to respond. Part of me wants to be irrational, but the other part wants to rationalize that it could happen; that we know nothing about the abomination or the process and reluctantly I lean away from him.

"There's something that I don't get," I say. "Why are you healing after biting me, but vampires have bit me before and they haven't changed back?"

He shakes his head. "I don't know. Maybe there's something different about the process of an abomination then a vampire. I mean, I know they're different..." He trails off, lost. "I just wish we had the answers."

"So do I." I glance back at the papers. "But we might be able to get some now."

He looks over at the papers curiously. "Is that why you came back here?" he asks and then a playfully asks, "or....was it to save me?"

I roll my eyes, but bite back a smile. "We came back for the papers... the one's you and I found before we were captured."

"So Aiden's going to help figure out what they say? So you can save the world? Save humanity?"

"No..." I'd almost forgotten about Aiden. "So you saw Aiden then?"

He nods, but seems reluctant. "During the chase, yeah, but not afterward... I just hope he hasn't been bitten."

I am not too sure that he is really concerned about Aiden being bit. The two brothers never did get along very well.

I sigh. "Well, even if he hasn't been bitten, he's still has changed."

He looks at me curiously. "What do you mean?"

I pick up my knife from the ground and hop up on the crates beside him. "He took the injection, Sylas."

He stares at me with his mouth agape. "He what? Why did he do it? He's always been against it… arguing with us about it. What the hell?"

"Because of me…Tristan told him what happened to us; that we were captured. He thought the only way he could save me… us, would be to become a Day Taker."

"He changed for *you*. To save you…" He considers this with a strange look on his face. "I'm glad he did."

He reaches out to lightly touch my cheek with his finger. I'm not sure how to react, be on guard or not, so I end up just sitting still.

He finally leans back, withdrawing his fingers from my cheek. "What else happened while I was gone?"

For some reason I'm hesitant to continue. I know that the both of them are competitive and I am afraid to tell Sylas *everything*. Especially that Aiden is a Day Walker not a Day Taker. I not sure how upset he'll be to hear it, and to hear that the power is going to Aiden's head, making him unstable.

Sylas senses my hesitation. "Whatever it is just say it."

Swallowing the lump in my throat I take a breath. "That injection didn't turn Aiden into a Day Taker. He's a Day Walker." There's hurt in his eyes, but it disappears rapidly as he tightens his jaw. "He also thinks that humans don't need to be saved," I add. "That the rest of the population needs to become Day Walkers because he feels they're *perfection*." I roll my eyes. "He thinks that the cure isn't the way we should be saving the world. That instead, we should be making people turn into Day Walkers, but only the people that we choose."

Sylas takes in everything that tell him, his expression serious. "If that's the case, then why did he come with you to get the papers?"

"I think he's hoping to change my mind. Make me agree with his ideas or something, but honestly, I don't know."

"Where is he now?"

"I don't know…" I glance at the crates around the room and the door; the only two things in here. "We got

147

separated when we were attacked by the monst—" I cut myself off, unsure what to call them since he was one of them—and he still sort of is.

"It's okay. They *are* monsters and I was one of them," he says like it's no big deal, but I feel the lies flowing off of him." They're all connected, you know. The monsters. Their thoughts, the movements they make, everything they do is connected. The Highers are intentionally creating them. Building an army."

My eyes enlarge. "An army? For what reason? They already control the vampires and the people in the colony. What do they need an army for?"

"They're not satisfied with what they have," he explains, picking at one of the wounds on his arms. "They want more. They know there are other people—humans— out there. They want to find them and take over there towns. Kill the ones who fight. But the thing that they really want," he pauses, looking up at me, "is you."

I sigh. "There's never enough for them. Greed. That's the reason it started and that's the reason it'll never end." I hop down from the crate. "Until I put a stop to it."

Sylas jumps down next to me, landing unsteadily on his feet. "How do you plan on stopping them exactly?" He sounds skeptical and it does seem impossible; however, I was created for a reason—to stop this.

Anger burns inside of me as I think of all the people that have either died or turned into some kind of monster because of the Highers' need for power. Their greed. They have ruined the world and made it a horrible place of death and fear. And what for? So they could have their rules; their control. Have everything. We have all simply walking around, obeying them, fearing them. But now it's time to change that; change the future.

"I plan on doing whatever it takes," I say, scooping up the papers, hoping they have the answers to the cure written upon them, knowing there's a chance they don't. I need to find a backup plan just in case something doesn't go right because I *will* save the world.

No matter what it takes.

Chapter 17

It takes the rest of the day for Sylas to finish changing back into himself. It's a painful process full of screaming and body shaking. His skin molts off, like feathers, and beneath it is rejuvenated skin. He's not wearing a shirt and keeps picking off pieces on his back, neck and chest, flicking them onto the floor. He seems to be gaining his strength back by the minute, breathing easier, moving lighter, like the Sylas I first met.

While we wait, I update him on everything that has happened. The escape, Nichelle, Maci falling from the cliff and about Mathew; how I need to take the papers back to him so he can help us find a cure. That he can read what's on the papers and maybe find a way to end the Highers' plan of greed once and for all.

"So other people and colonies really do exist." He muses at this, rubbing his jawline, pacing back and forth in front of the crates I'm sitting on to stretch out his legs. He said they feel extremely stiff from being crooked and bent and it's sort of hard for him to walk.

"I'm guessing that's why the Highers are creating their army... they don't want to risk anyone becoming more powerful than them." He stops pacing and stands directly in front of me. "So they'll send the monsters out to gain their control and kill."

"It makes sense," I admit, reaching forward and peeling a stray piece of skin off his arm. "They don't want the chance of an uprising, so they send abominations to take control of the cities and kill any people who try to resist."

"I'm guessing that you and I are onto something." He smiles amusedly at me while picking off one last strip of skin from his stomach. He looks completely normal. "You know what," he flicks the piece of skin onto the ground, "I feel so much better now."

I flip the knife around in my hand, playing with it. "You look better now."

"Better?" he asks with a crook of his brow. "Or sexy?"

I roll my eyes, but my stomach flips. "Glad you haven't lost your sense of humor."

"You know you've missed it." He waits, his silence challenging me to say otherwise. When I don't answer, I've pretty much agreed he's right.

I'm not sure how I feel about that.

"We should probably get going if you're feeling better and it should be dark by now." I hop off the crates and put the knife away. "There's no point sitting around and wasting time." I walk over and pick up the papers.

Sylas glances around the room. "I need a shirt or something."

"Well, where did you get the pants?"

His eyes darken. "You don't even want to know."

He's probably right, so I take off my jacket and toss it to him. He catches it and puts it on. It's large on me, but still a little too small on him. He manages to get it zipped up then we head out a door that leads to the outside. We're on high alert as we watch for abominations. Although, I now know how to change Sylas back if he gets bit, I'd rather keep the getting bit on my part low.

Sylas grabs the door handle behind him, but pauses. "What about Aiden?"

I pause, deliberating what the right thing to do is. "Um... I guess we should probably find him."

"Are you sure?" he questions. "You do realize that the Highers are probably searching for us, right? They have a connection with their army and will probably know that you are here right now.... Plus, they'll probably figure out that I'm no longer with their group of soldiers and search for me because I know stuff."

"You think they know that you reversed back to a Day Taker?"

He shrugs. "I'm not sure. But if they do figure it out and find out that you're the reason why I've changed, *you* will definitely become their top priority." He lets go of the doorknob and takes hold of my hand, his skin temperature matching mine "You've got to promise to be cautious. If the Highers get their hands on you... well, they'll have what they need to become what they've always strived to be. Perfection."

"Then I'll just have to make sure they don't get their hands on me," I tell him determinedly.

"*We'll* make sure," he presses, his dark eyes turning to liquid black like the ink on the papers that I'm holding. "*We'll* make sure that they don't get their hands on you."

"You know, you sound like your good at the moment," I say in a light tone.

The corners of his lips quirk. "Don't tell anyone. I have a reputation to uphold."

He lets go of my hands and then we head out the door, checking the hallway before stepping out. It's silent as we back our way down the hallway, the only noises are the soft flaps coming from the plastic above us and the crunching as we step on debris. I follow him down the hall, folding up the papers the best that I can, then reach forward to put them into the jacket pocket that Sylas is wearing. He tenses and freezes from my touch, startled. When he glances at me, I shrug.

"I don't want to be holding them if we have to run," I say.

He stares at my hand as I pull away and then, when he looks up, he has this strange look in his eyes. He reaches forward and tucks a strand of my hair out of my eyes before turning away and heading up the hall again.

When we reach the end, the hall exits to the outside through a hole in the wall. We slip into the shadows of the night, carefully treading through the park to the dark streets, keeping to the alleys while listening to the vampire cries around us.

Sylas pauses for a moment when we reach a corner of a building and then sticks out his hand behind him, grabs hold of me and pulls me forward. I step up to the side of him as he puts his fingers to his lips, warning me to stay quiet, then he peeks around the corner and motions for me to do the same. I lean around him and look into the street. There are fires burning in barrels everywhere and three figures standing next to one of the closer fires, wearing all white that matches their hair. Their snow-white skin carves their perfect features and their pale eyes are haunting.

Highers.

I can't hear what they're saying, but I want to; I want to see if they're talking about something that could clue us in on what they know. I start to sidestep around Sylas, wanting to get closer, when he catches my arm, but I shake my head and point to my ear. He hesitates then lets me go, following on my heels. We stick to the shadows and then duck behind a rusted vehicle on the street, just out of the glow flowing off the flames in the barrels.

Gabrielle's voice rises and I tense, recognizing the sound of it far too well. I strain my ears to listen, hunkering low at the same time Sylas sits down on the rubbly street with his legs out.

"We need to send our army out," he says. "Now that we know where some of the humans are hiding."

"If Kayla gets the papers back to Mathew," another one says, his voice is unfamiliar, but it holds the same icy tone, "eventually they'll be able to figure out Monarch's work. He'll be able to figure out the cure."

It grows quiet and I dare to peek up through the cracked window of the car. Gabrielle's peering around the dark streets, his pale eyes ultimately resting on the rusted vehicle we're hiding behind. I hold my breath, thinking he knows we're there, but then he turns back to the other Highers.

"It's more important to find her first, so we can capture her," a Higher says. He looks familiar, but I can't quite place why. "It'll take some time for Mathew to decipher my work and we need her blood more than anything."

I gasp when I realize Monarch is speaking and then slap my hand over my mouth. Sylas reaches up and pulls me back down, shaking his head at me.

"You need to stay down," he hisses.

He's right. I can't allow my emotions to make me become reckless. I was trained not to.

"How do they know about the papers?" Sylas whispers. "And if they did, why didn't they just pick them up to begin with and destroy them."

"I have no idea." I pause. "Unless someone told them."

Gabrielle and Monarch grow silent but then a shuffling sound causes Sylas to lean forward, carefully peeking around the corner from our hiding spot, ready to bolt if we have to. However, they're still standing in the same spot, in a circle, Monarch and Gabrielle in the center.

"How do we even know that Aiden is telling us the truth?" Gabrielle sneers. My eyes widen as I feel Sylas tense beside me, his fingers brushing mine. *Aiden? He was talking to the Highers? Was he the one who told them about the papers?* I hate to think it, but he has to be.

"Aiden's been programed by me since he was a small boy," Monarch replies, swishing his robe behind him as he moves over beside the fire, peering at it. "Just like all of the children, he can't lie to me, even when he fights it. He can try all he wants, but in the end, he tells the truth against his own free will without even understanding what he's doing. He was telling the truth about the town and the papers." He pauses and tears his eyes away from the fire, looking at the darkness around him. "And we'll know in a few days what will happen to Aiden."

"As I said before, we need to send our armies in and have them take over the town," Gabrielle says in a low voice as he walks up beside Monarch. "We need to bring all the people back to us before Kayla returns there. We'll have Mathew as our prisoner and without him, Kayla won't understand how to make the cure."

"You know that we can't execute that command on our own," Monarch says, turning to face Gabrielle. The two stand tall, rising to each other's height, like they're both trying to be commander, and the rest of the Highers hover back and watch. They looks almost the same, hair like snow, eyes that match, and I wonder if the man that I once thought of as my father is even in there anymore or if he's dead.

"We must present it to the rest of the Highers and it must meet their approval. Rules. Remember?" Monarch asks.

"That could take days," Gabrielle growls. "Even weeks."

"We go by rules and order for a reason," Monarch reminds him. "Everyone agrees, or we don't proceed."

Gabrielle considers this for a long time, with the fires crackling the only backdrop noise. "Fine." Gabrielle sounds angry, yet he agrees. "But we need to do it quickly. I want the army sent out as soon as possible, so that the humans are caught off guard."

Monarch nods and then they hurry off in the opposite direction toward where the street narrows with the other Highers following behind them. I wait until they're gone before I sit back down behind the car on the ground covered in ash drifting from the burning barrels.

There's silence between us, neither of us knowing what to say about any of this—about Aiden.

"What do you think Monarch meant when he said that they'd know in a few days what was going to happen to Aiden?" I finally dare ask Sylas.

Sylas shakes his head as he stares out at the dark street in front of us, lined with broken cars. "I don't know, but apparently Aiden told them everything he knew about Mathew…. and the cure." His tone is tinged with anger.

"It wasn't Aiden's fault," I say, because it's not. I know what it's like to be controlled like that. "You can't blame him. Monarch said he programmed him to obey him and not to lie to him." I always felt that Monarch cared about me. How wrong I had been to believe that. He was and always would be nothing, except a liar. A fake.

A Higher.

"This is bad, Sylas. We can't let them send their army to that colony. Those people will be an easy target for the Highers and I left Maci and Greyson there... and if they capture Mathew, there's going to be no hope left for a cure." I blow out a stressed breath, thinking of poor Maci and how she's injured. I thought I was keeping her safe by leaving her there, but now I'm not so sure.

"Then we need to leave now if we want to beat them there," Sylas tells me, his eyes burning with determination. "We'll have to let Aiden take care of himself."

"But—"

He holds up his hand, cutting me off. "You have to let him go... you can't save everyone, Kayla."

I feel queasy as a memory surfaces in my thoughts.

"You need to learn to let go of your emotions, Kayla," Monarch tells me, sitting beside me on the floor. "You can't let yourself become attached to people."

"But what about Sylas and Aiden?" I ask. "I don't want anything to happen to them."

Monarch looks disappointed in me. *"There are other things more important than Sylas and Aiden. Much bigger things, and there will come a time when you'll have to choose your battles; to let someone go. You need to realize that you can't save everyone. Not if you are going to save the world."* He pauses. *"Do you understand what I'm saying?"*

I nod. *"Yes, I understand. Getting the cure and saving the world is the most important thing,"* I answer robotically.

He gives me a small smile, but his eyes are filled with remorse. *"Good girl,"* he says and then pats my head

I lean back against the wall as he injects my arm with a needle. I've gotten so used to it that I barely feel the sting. My vision grows blurry as his voice fades.

"I just hope you'll remember this when the time comes," I hear him say and then I slip into unconsciousness.

I blink my eyes. Sylas is snapping his fingers in front of my face. I shake my head as I look at him.

"Having another memory flashback?" he asks me, brushing ash out of his hair.

I glance around in the steel buildings, listening to the cries of the vampires from somewhere in the distance. "Yeah, and I think you are right. We'll have to leave Aiden for now." I hate saying it, but it feels right. "We need to get these papers back to Mathew and help them before the Highers' army arrives." I get to my feet and brush my hands down the back of my jeans, dusting off the dirt.

Sylas stands to his feet as I turn around and then we make our way back through the streets lined with barrels and vampires, heading towards Mathew and the colony. We move as fast as we can with the vampires' screams piercing the air all around us, winding around cars, leaping over them, knowing we have to hurry. My only hope is that we make it back before the Highers' army gets there.

That we can save the world before it's too late.

Chapter 18

The cold night air feels like it should be affecting me, slowing me down or hindering my endurance, but it doesn't. I never get tired and Sylas keeps up with me easily. It's kind of perfect running through the desert at my own speed.

"This is fun," Sylas says as we hop over rocks.

"You think?" I leap over a large rock and land gracefully on the other side.

He drops down beside me and smiles. "I do. In fact, I think we should do it more often."

I don't answer, however I smile as we race off again. We're just on the outskirts of the colony, feeling good about how fast we're moving, when we cross a herd of vampires in our path. They're wandering around, trying to find something to feed on, with their heads tipped back towards the sky, crying out.

I slam to a halt when I notice them and draw out my knife, ready to attack. I know that the vampires are afraid of me, but Sylas's scent might attract them. He slows down beside me, starting to ask what I'm doing, but then he turns his head and his eyes slightly widen as he sees them and he steps back.

One of the vampires glances over at us and then the rest smell the air.

"Sylas, run," I order as I stick my hand out to protect him.

He doesn't budge and I'm about to shove him back when the vampires suddenly lower their heads and cower back. A braver one comes running up towards us, but then it veers quickly to the right and leaves with the others.

I give Sylas a puzzled look from over my shoulder and he shrugs.

"They probably caught your scent," he says, yet he doesn't sound completely convinced. We've been attacked before together. My scent doesn't always repel them so easily.

Still, I nod and then we start running again down the path and over the hill to the outskirts of where the vampires have migrated. It's like we're herding them away, forcing them to run.

Every once in a while, one will turn back towards Sylas like it's about to attack him, but then quickly darts forward like it's afraid. They head out to the flat land and finally they're a safe distance away.

I stop and so does Sylas, watching them cry in the distance. He looks at me funny and then we continue to walk. "Maybe my scent isn't normal," he says with a confused look on his face. "Well, normal for me."

"What do you mean?" I ask as I hop from a large rock to a smaller one.

He matches my move breezily. "Well, think about it. I had changed into an abomination. The vampires are afraid of them. Maybe I still have the same smell as when I was changed."

"You could be right, but if that's the case, I wonder if it will be permanent."

"Maybe. I wonder if there's a cure for that."

"Do you want there to be a cure for that?" I ask. "It's kind of convenient."

He wavers. "Yeah, I guess, but still… those things smell disgusting." He sniffs himself and pulls a puzzled face. "I honestly can't smell anything, except dirt."

I lean over and sniff his chest. "You smell fine to me."

He bites his bottom lip as I lean away. I can tell that he wants to do something to me; maybe kiss me like he did back when he was changing. I take off before he can do so, knowing I could easily get caught up in his kisses. He jogs after me, smiling to himself.

We maintain a rapid pace and make it back to the cave before daylight. Sylas insists that he can make the rest of the journey in the daylight and that he'll keep his jacket on to protect himself. I argue for a moment then I hear Monarch's words echoing in my head once more.

There are other things more important than Sylas and Aiden. You need to realize that you can't save everyone. Not if you are going to save the world.

His words haunt me. I shake my head to try and clear it, but it doesn't work and I hear them again.

There are other things more important than Sylas and Aiden. You need to realize that you can't save everyone. Not if you are going to save the world.

"You're right, we should keep going," I tell him, not liking myself that much at the moment.

His lips curve to a pleased grin. "I think you are finally starting to understand what you need to do."

"Maybe." *Or maybe Monarch's just stuck in my head.*

Sylas draws his hood over his head and tucks his hands up into his sleeves. We start moving again as the sunlight casts against our backs. Sylas slows down a little, but not enough that it makes me feel like I'm lagging. Finally, after racing around rocks, going uphill and downhill, we arrive at the colony.

There are two guards posted on top of the wall created from scraps of car. It's the same two that were there when Aiden and I left. They stand up on the wall, pointing their knives at us as we approach.

"Stop where you are, both of you," the guard closest to us threatens, raising his knife in a threatening manner.

Sylas and I both stop at the bottom of the wall and stare up at them. The one guard hops down in front of us, landing with a grunt, then holds his weapon out as he circles around us.

He walks up to me, eyes roving my long, black hair and short height. "I remember you. You're that Kayla creature that left here not too long ago." He eyes me over again as Sylas's jaw tightens and he inches closer to me protectively. "Mathew told us that we're supposed to let you back in when you return."

His scrutinizing gaze diverts to Sylas. He aims the tip of the knife at his chest. I'm worried Sylas will retaliate, however he tips his head down away from the sun.

"But you're not the same guy who was here before," the guard says suspiciously. He pauses. "He can wait here. We don't know what he is or what he wants." He shoves the weapon into Sylas's chest and the blade glazes through the fabric of my jacket he has on.

Before I can blink, Sylas smashes his elbow into the guard's face then, without missing a beat, he thrusts his knee into his wrist, steals the knife and flips it around so it's aimed at the bewildered guard's face.

The guard on the top of the barricade lets out a scream and then I hear the sound of a ringing bell. I'm not even sure where the hell it's coming from, but I hear a rustle of commotion from the other side of the barricade. Sylas continues to stand, pointing the weapon at the guard's throat who doesn't dare move. The other guard jumps down and points his knife at Sylas.

I'm deciding whether to knock Sylas out or the guards—what would make things easier—when Mathew arrives at the top of the wall. He peers down at us with his pale eyes, taking in the situation, then turns and very unsteadily climbs down. The guard with the weapon aimed at Sylas says something to him in a low tone when he approaches us.

Mathew shakes his head and shoves away the knife the guard's holding then smiles at me. "I'm glad you made it back and that you brought Sylas with you."

Sylas is startled, but he still keeps his head down because he has to. "How do you know my name?"

He ignores Sylas's question, eying the knife in Sylas's hand still pointed at the guard. "Let me apologize for the way the guards treated you. Sometimes they get a little too protective of our town, but then again, I can't blame them."

Sylas hesitates, his muscles stiff, then finally he turns the weapon back around and hands it to the guard with an irritated look on his face.

"I'll let it go this time," Sylas says in a low tone. Even though I can't see his eyes from below his hood, the warning in his tone causes even me to shiver. "But next time I won't."

The guard takes the weapon, glaring at him, yet he doesn't say a word. He quickly climbs back up the wall and the other guard follows.

Mathew motions for us to follow him and we all climb up the wall and down the other side. As we move, I notice that Mathew looks different then when I saw him just a couple of days ago. His eyes and skin seems to be much more pallid and he really struggles to get up that wall. *I wonder if he is starting to change faster now.*

Mathew picks up his walking stick and then we head down a dirt path towards a building. "Did you find the papers, Kayla?" He looks at me inquisitively, waiting for my response.

I pat Sylas's pocket. "They're right here," I tell him.

Relief floods across his face as his legs shake in the attempt to bear his weight. "Good. Let's hurry inside my lab and see if I can make sense out of them."

The word lab sends a red flag up in my head and apparently in Sylas, too, because he slams to a stop, grabbing my arm and pulling me back.

"Wait just a minute... you knew my name..." He trails off, muttering under his breath. "Yet you can't really see my face beneath the hood."

"Because I could tell who you were," a familiar voice rises behind us, causing Sylas and I to spin around.

My jaw drops at the sight of Aiden standing behind us with his hood pulled down and a dark smile on his face. "Glad to see you're back to your old self, brother."

Aiden stares at us as we remain silent, looking back and forth between the two of us like he's waiting for us to say something. We don't because we don't know what to say; what's going on? Why is he here? Does he remember telling Monarch about the papers? Or maybe he doesn't even understand any of this?

"Aren't you glad to see me?" he asks.

I manage a fake smile, deciding that I'll play along until I figure out what's going on. "Of course I am, but... what happened to you? Sylas and I tried to find you after we were separated."

"I managed to escape the abominations," he says. "I went back to the cave and waited, but when you didn't show up, I decided that maybe I missed you and you'd come back here." He gestures at the town that surrounds us. "So I came back, too."

I'm not buying it at all, though at the same time, maybe that's what he thinks really happened. Especially after what I heard Monarch say to Gabrielle in the street about him telling the truth against his own free will.

Aiden assesses Sylas with his brows dipped together. "I thought you changed into an abomination?"

"Apparently, their bite doesn't change Day Takers like we thought," Sylas lies. "All that happened was that I got sick... Kayla found me hiding inside one of the buildings."

He looks skeptical as sunlight bathes over him, reminding me what he is. "Well, it's good to know that you're both safe... and alive."

Mathew clears his throat behind us. "I don't mean to break up this little reunion, but I really need to get to work on the cure if we want to have any hope of deciphering it."

He doesn't wait for an answer from any of us; he simply turns and walks across the path towards a two-story brick building that has two more guards by the door.

Sylas and I follow him with Aiden trailing behind us, making me uneasy and on high alert. I'm not sure what's going on; if he's good, bad—what the hell he is at the moment, since he's always all over the place.

The guards look at us from the corners of their eyes as we walk by, but do not bother us. Mathew leads us inside of the building where we walk down a narrow hallway and into a room at the end, a few guards following at our heels. Everything inside the room is white, and there are glass shelves with bottles of some liquid on them. It reminds me of the room Monarch worked in; the one where I received all of my injections. I tense when I realize this.

There's a table in the center of the room, shiny and made of metal, which Mathew walks over to. "Can I see the papers?"

I glance at Sylas, wondering what we should do. He wavers, looking at Aiden and then at Mathew, knowing we don't have much time. I can tell that both Aiden and this room are making him nervous. Still, he takes the papers out of his pocket and puts them down on the table.

Mathew picks up the stack of papers and thumbs through them. He shakes his head starts placing them into separate stacks. As he does this, Aiden looks around the room, seeming bored, while Sylas watches Aiden with a look that says if he makes one move, Sylas will hurt Aiden badly. The problem is, I'm not so sure Sylas is stronger than Aiden anymore.

"There, that should do it," Mathew says. He quickly picks up the stack of papers and starts reading them over.

"I'm going to need a bit of time to go through these." He has an intense look on his face as he reads whatever's on them. "You might want to go check on Maci, Kayla. She was asking for you." He sets one of the pieces of papers down. "She's in the next building over."

I'm hesitant, yet I still exit the room, knowing I should go check up on Maci and Greyson. Aiden and Sylas both continue to hover near Mathew, each refusing to leave, then at the same time, they both turn towards me. Sylas follows me out, however Aiden continues to hang back, his eyes focused on the papers that are spread out upon the table. Even though I'm hesitant to leave Mathew alone with the papers, I'd feel better if Aiden wasn't around him.

"Aiden, are you coming with us?" I ask in the fakest polite tone I can muster up because there's no way I'm leaving him here with Mathew.

Aiden glances over at me, eyes cold, but walks after us. Suddenly, I can breathe freer.

That is, until he stops and says, "I'm just going to wait here until Mathew is done... I'm not sure if we can trust him anymore."

"Or is it because you want the papers?" I ask. "After all that stuff you were saying back at Cell 7, I'm not so sure I can trust you."

"You can trust me," he says. I can't tell if he's lying or not. "But I have to say that I'm sort of hurt that you don't seem happy that I made it back here okay."

"I am," I lie. "How did you make it back, though? How did you escape the abominations so easily?" I want to say something that will allow me to see if he's lying, whether he's really bad or if deep down he's still good, yet under the control of Monarch.

Aiden gives me a dry smile, like he can see right through my bullshit. "I ran." He's telling the truth.

"And you didn't run into any problems along the way?" I ask.

He shakes his head, seeming confused. "No... well, other than those abominations. It was a pain in the ass to escape them."

I shake my head, frustrated, because everything he's saying is true. I move to head to the door, but Sylas doesn't follow, so I stop and turn back around.

He keeps his eyes on Aiden. "You know what; I think I'll keep my brother company."

Aiden shrugs. "Okay, if you want to."

Sylas casts a glance at me then slides down onto the hallway floor, leaning back against the brick wall, giving me a look that lets me know he'll keep an eye on things before returning his attention to his brother. "I haven't seen you since I was captured. We have a lot of catching up to do, don't you think?"

Aiden nods and then sits down across from him. I reluctantly leave them and hurry out the exit door at the end, wanting to check up on things quickly so I can get back, wanting to be near the papers so I'll know they're okay. Two guards standing there with knives in their hands watch me as I hurry past them and out onto the path. I pause as I stare at the few buildings in the area; I can't tell which one Maci's supposed to be in.

I glance back at the guards. "Can you tell me where Maci and Greyson are by chance?"

The guards gape at me blankly. "Who are you talking about?" The taller, more slender one with brown hair says.

"The little girl that came here with me... she fell off a cliff and was hurt," I say, unsure if they know what I'm talking about.

A flash of recognition crosses the slender one's face. "Is that what happened to her?" he sneers. "Or was it something you Day Takers did to her?"

I'm not in the mood for this shit anymore. I take a slow, measured step closer to him with my arms to my sides, my shoulders square. He cowers back against the wall—they both do. "If you know what a Day Taker is, then you know what I can do," I say in a firm tone. "So shut up and point the way to where I can find Maci and Greyson."

His finger shakes as he points it to a small stucco building across the path, nestled beside another building and some trees. I turn away and make my way over to the building, resisting the urge to go back and punch him in the face. I can't help noticing the people I pass by. Most of them are either staring at me or whispering to each other, feelings of hate and fear radiating from them as they quickly jump out of my way, clearing a path for me. I can't help wondering why I'm trying to save people. They despise and fear anything that is different from them. Then I remember the words Aiden said to me earlier.

If everyone's the same, then how can someone be considered perfect when there's no imperfection to compare them to?

What am I doing thinking that way? I shake the thoughts out of my head and walk to the stucco building the guards pointed to, people continuing to clear out of my way until I have open land in front of me. When I reach the door, I can hear voices giggling from inside, which makes me feel just a little bit better.

I open the door and walk inside, immediately startled. Maci is sitting inside with about a dozen other children while, at the front of the small room, is a young woman with blondish hair streaked with blue that matches her pants. She has black boots on and a white button-up shirt. She's telling some kind of story to the children about something called ponies and a lot of rainbows.

The room is actually pretty colorful; the walls this alarming shade of green and covered with pieces of paper that have drawings on them.

The children are all smiling at her as they listen to the story, and in the middle of the crowd, is a red headed girl.

Maci. She looks like she's enjoying herself. When she turns in my direction, she jumps up from her seat, smiling.

"You're here!" she exclaims, running over and wrapping her arms around me. The rest of the children follow her, looking equally as happy. I'm shocked when they circle around me, joining in the hug Maci offers me.

I'm instantly reminded why I need to save the world again.

Chapter 19

The young woman in the room tells the children that they need to sit back down. I look up at her, expecting to see her eyes filled with hate like the rest of the people in the colony, so I'm surprised when she smiles at me with kindness in her eyes.

Maci grabs my hand and pulls me towards the door. "Come on, Kayla. We need to talk."

She leads me outside the door and around to the back of the building. There's an alleyway that is surrounded by walls and the only way out is the way we came in. Then Maci lets go of my hand and starts humming as she skips around in a circle.

"Why did you bring me out here?" I ask her as I look around the empty alley.

"Because I am supposed to." She shrugs as she kicks at some pebbles on the ground.

As usual, I'm confused at what she's talking about. "Can you tell me why you're supposed to?"

"Not yet," she says. "But soon."

I sigh. *I wish she could just tell us what we're supposed to do instead of letting us know she knows. Things would be so much simpler.* "What were you doing back in that building?"

She stops skipping and her eyes light up with excitement. "That was a school. They teach the children how to read there."

"They teach people to read here?" I ask, stunned.

She nods her head with enthusiasm. "They teach lots of things Kayla. It's different from our colony where the Highers are always controlling things and hiding things."

"I don't doubt that," I tell her. "Since they don't have Highers here."

The sound of yelling suddenly interrupts us. I wonder if this is why Maci brought me back here, to hear something. The yelling is coming from around the corner, in front of the building. I start to take off to see what the commotion is about, but Maci grabs my arm and draws me back.

"You need to stay here," she tells me. I shake my head, worried it's the army or something, and then I begin to pull away. "Kayla, listen to me," Maci says. "You *have* to stay here. They're yelling because of you."

I listen to the yells and suddenly I comprehend what she is telling me. They want to lock me away because they're afraid of me.

"They don't hate you," she says sadly. "They just don't understand you. They don't know how important you are."

"I hope you're right," I mutter, trying to block out the hateful words from the street, but it's hard.

"I am," she says simply.

The yelling continues for a while and then their voices suddenly fade. I hear Mathew speak, telling everyone to quiet down.

"We can go out now," Maci whispers quietly, motioning me to go.

I cautiously make my way back to the front of the building and find Mathew standing on top of the steps of the building. Sylas is standing beside him with his hood remaining over his head because there's still sunlight. The people in the crowd are all staring at Sylas as if he is some sort of a monster. I can tell by the look in their eyes what they're feeling. Fear. They want to kill Sylas. And possibly me.

This is bad.

Mathew is trying to calm them down, but the colony members are still uneasy. I take a deep breath and start to walk towards Mathew and Sylas. When I step out from around the corner, many people turn in my direction and the crowd begins to murmur again. I ignore their angry looks and walk with my chin held high up the steps and stand beside Sylas. He glances at me and then discreetly moves his covered hand over and slips his fingers through mine.

"Everyone needs to calm down. Sylas and Kayla are not responsible for what happened. I wasn't attacked by them." Mathew's voice echoes over the crowd. I wonder what the hell he's talking about. "Sylas is the one who saved me from Aiden. He went up against his own brother to protect me," Mathew explains and my eyes widen in shock.

What did I miss?

Sylas must sense my confusion because he squeezes my hand, and even though I hate to admit it, I find it comforting. Mathew steps down to the bottom of the stairway and into the crowd of people. He immediately gets bombarded with questions about what happened; where the other one is, what he's going to do about the problem. They look at us every time they say problem and it irks me to my very core.

"What is going on?" I whisper, leaning in towards Sylas.

"I guess Aiden put thoughts into people's heads and made them do things," he whispers back. "He tried to get me to attack Mathew, but was surprised when I didn't respond. When his little gift didn't work on me, he tried to get me to tell him why. I honestly have no idea why it didn't work on me, but the next thing I knew, he bit me... He was able to see my thoughts." He swallows hard with his head bowed down. "He knows that you changed me back, Kayla."

I notice there are a few drops of blood on his jacket; however the wound on his neck has started to heal, barely two specks.

"And it gets worse," Sylas continues. "His bite made me black out for a few minutes and that's when he attacked Mathew. I managed to pull him off before he bit him and then he ran off... with the papers." He pauses, shaking his head at himself. "I don't get it... I used to be so much stronger than him, but felt so helpless... he took out the guards, too…" He shakes his head again and tips his chin up, keeping his eyes angled from the sun. "He's different. Stronger than anything I've ever come across. I think he might really be working for the Highers."

I swallow hard, wondering why I felt Monarch lying to Gabrielle when he clearly was telling the truth. The crowd starts to break up and Mathew walks back up the stairs towards us with a strange look on his face that makes me tense even more.

"I think I know the reason he attacked me," Mathew says as he reaches the top of the stairway and stands in front of us.

"Because of the papers," I say. "I think that the Highers have him brainwashed somehow."

Mathew shakes his head. "Not brainwashed." He pauses, gazing out at the sun descending below the mountains. "Aiden's changing into a Higher."

"What!" Sylas and I both cry simultaneously.

Sylas inches closer, anger surfacing in his expression as he dares to look up from the ground just the slightest bit. "How can you be so sure?"

Mathew shuts his eyes, puts his hand into his pockets and then takes a piece of paper out before opening his eyes. "I managed to read quite a bit before he stole the papers... I even had this one in my hand when he attacked me." He unfolds the paper. "Monarch says on this one that he messed up on subject 409, a boy named Aiden. That he broke the DNA... put too much of injection 7 in him..." He trails off as Sylas and I gape at him, having no idea what he's talking about. "Right." He stuffs the paper back into his pocket. "To make a long story short, Kayla is the only perfect soldier. As much as Monarch tried, he couldn't create anything like her. He had a few failed attempts where he created something else—something almost perfect—yet filled with one flaw, greed. A Higher; and Aiden was one of them he messed up on."

Sylas lets go of my hand and turns away. As much as the brothers fought, I can tell this is affecting him. He stands there for a moment, and when he looks at me, there's a hint of sadness on his face, something I've never seen on him before. He erases it, though, and then shifts his attention back to Mathew.

"So Aiden stole the papers to prevent you from finding the cure?" he asks, drawing his hood back as the last of the sunlight slips away and the sky turns grey. I can hear faint howling in the distance start. "Does that mean there is no hope for a cure?"

"Not necessarily," Mathew says, glancing around at the people in the streets rushing inside. "I think I read enough information before the papers were taken. I might understand what needs to happen to establish a cure. I just need some time to process it all... think... put stuff together."

I look over at Sylas; the worry on his face matches the way that I feel. Time. I'd almost forgotten. We probably don't have much time.

Taking a breath, I turn back to Mathew. "When we were in the colony, we heard the Highers talking about the monsters they've created; the ones we call abominations. They're sending out an army of them out to find humans and bring them back."

Mathew gapes at us, his wide eyes matching the full moon in the backdrop. "They're coming *here*? To our town?"

"I think so," I tell him. "At least, that's what we've heard… although they said it could take days, even weeks to get the orders through."

Mathew glances around at the streets winding in and out of the buildings, panicking, probably visualizing the madness and chaos that could happen. They're fairly empty now, but they were packed quite a while ago, and if the abominations were around, they'd have chased down every last one.

He looks at both Sylas and me, pleading. "Can you help us?"

This town was ready to lock us up, yet Mathew wants us to protect them—save them. Sylas glances at me, and I can tell he's thinking the same thing, waiting to see what I tell Mathew. Monarch told me I was here to help find a cure. That my purpose was to save humanity. To save the world.

"That's what I was made for," I say, my thoughts sort of connect, forming an understanding.

I understand. What I have to do. What I am. Why I was created.

Mathew breathes a sigh of relief. "Thank you."

"Don't thank us yet," Sylas says. "Just because we'll help you, doesn't mean we'll win," he states bluntly. When Mathew frowns, he adds, "Just gather everyone that can fight."

He nods his head and walks away down the street, heading towards the guards near the closest building.

"Do you think that I'm doing the right thing?" I ask Sylas. "Do you think I'm even strong enough to help?"

"I think that you're doing what you are supposed to do." He takes my hand and offers me a smile. A real one, too, which he's rarely—if ever—done.

I open my mouth to say more because I'm worried about if I can handle this, but he silences me by placing his lips on mine. His tongue slips between my lips. He tastes so good that I open my mouth and willingly let him explore me. We don't notice when Maci walks up behind us until she taps me on the side.

We break away from each other, startled. Or at least I am. Sylas looks momentarily content.

"It's time," Maci announces with her hands on her hips.

"Time for what?" I ask her, wondering if I'm going to get another one of her little riddles about the future.

"Time for me to tell you how to save the world," she answers.

Chapter 20

What in the world? Sylas and I stare at her, stunned.

The grey sky darkens with each second that goes by until it's jet black, but the glow of torches on the buildings lining the silent street radiates around us. The temperature has descended and more and more cries circle the town as more vampires awaken for the night.

"What do you mean?" I finally ask Maci. Sylas glances at me, his face contorted in confusion. "I thought you weren't supposed to tell us anything like that?"

"I told you when the time was right I would tell you," she says with a cheerful, small smile, her red hair blowing in the breeze. "And the time is finally right."

She turns her attention to Sylas, tipping her head back so she can look at him. "You need to go and get the other Day Takers and bring them here. It's the only way things will work."

He's not looking at her, but at me, gaping incredulously. "What's she talking about?"

"I'm talking about saving the world," Maci answers. "So please just get going."

Sylas gradually turns in her direction, his eyelids lowering as he glares at her. "And how the hell do you know anything?"

"Sylas," I warn, taking his arm, slightly worried at what he might do. "Maci's usually right about these things."

He studies her with wariness. "But she's just a little kid."

"A little kid that knows more than you." Maci glares at him, crossing her arms. "And you need to go now before it's too late."

Sylas is shocked because he isn't used to taking orders. "Are you telling me what to do?" He points at himself, flabbergasted.

"Yeah," Maci answers with attitude. "And if you know what's good for you, then you'll listen."

Sylas rolls his eyes. "I won't take orders from a little kid."

"Will you take them from me then?" I ask because I know Maci has to be right. If she says the Day Takers need to be here, then they need to be here.

Sylas turns to face me, pushing up the sleeves of his jacket, his lean muscles flexing as he crosses them. "Have I ever taken orders from anyone?"

"I'm not giving you orders," I sigh. "I'm asking you to go."

He continues to keeps his attention focused on me, and it's hard not to look away, yet at the same time, not impossible. I maintain his gaze, hoping he'll cave and realize this isn't about who gets to give orders.

"Fine," he relents and then surprises me when he leans over and gives me a quick, though passionate, kiss; stealing the breath right out of my lungs and making my lips swell. When he pulls away, he looks dazed, but I'm not sure if it's because of the kiss or because he's taking orders from a child. "I'll hurry back as fast as I can... but it's going to take me a while to gather them and bring them back."

"Do you have to go back to the city?"

"I'm not sure," he says with a simple shrug as he shuffles towards the stairway. "If they followed the orders I gave Emmy, then they'll be at the Grates... but you never know with Day Takers since they hate taking orders." He flashes me a cocky smile.

"Be safe," I tell him. He gives me a look as if to say 'no duh'.

"Of course, Juniper," he says, winking at me when he uses my nickname. "I always am."

He starts to step down the stairway towards the street, but pauses at the bottom to glance up at me one last time. For a brief second, he looks afraid, and for a fleeting moment, I feel the same way. Then he turns, and I watch him race off at inhuman speed until he vanishes out of the glow of the torches.

I turn my attention back to Maci, feeling my stomach burn, knowing the last time we split that terrible things happened. "So, what do I need to do?"

She points to our right to where the street curves up a shallow hill. "You need to protect Mathew."

"Just Mathew?" I ask. "What about the rest of the people?"

"Kayla, go find Mathew and talk to him," she says. "Then you will understand."

I want to question her more, however I know better than to do so. She's pretty much been correct with everything that she has told me previously, so after I drop her off at the building, with the woman teaching the children, I hurry off down the street to find Mathew. I make it next to the building where the lab is when I run into Nichelle. There's a small group of people with her, wearing all black, and they all are armed with a knives, sticks, spears and even a few swords. They look like average people dressed up in fighting gear that are creating the illusion that they can fight. I know it's not real because beneath their armor I can hear their hearts racing with fear.

We're doomed.

They're doomed.

When does they're become a we?

"Mathew said that we were supposed to find you," Nichelle tells me. Her hair is pulled up in a bun and she the boots she is wearing go up to her knees. There's this strange black band around her neck with a small metal pouch hooked to it. "Poison," she says.

I'm confused. "What?"

She points at her neck at the collar and the pouch. "I saw you looking at it and I can tell you're wondering what it is." She lifts up a hook on the pouch and beneath it is a pin-size button. "If I get bit, I push this and it injects my veins with poison that will kill me before the virus takes over my body."

"So you'd rather die than change?" I've heard Sylas say this, but it's surprising to hear humans are the same way, too; that we both feel the same way.

She nods. "Wouldn't you?"

I nod. "I would."

There's a pause where we realize we're not so different. Then Nichelle clears her throat.

"Anyway, Mathew said you'd show us where each of us needs to be so we can protect the town," she says with an eye roll. "He thinks you're going to save the town somehow—that you're a better fighter than me—but he's wrong."

She'd think differently if she ever saw me in action.

"You know the town better than me." I glance around at the unfamiliar structures and alleys around me; I don't even know where any of them lead to. "You should be in charge of getting everyone into position."

She nods, satisfied, and then starts to walk away when I snag her by the jacket sleeve and pull her back to me. "Sylas will be coming back sometime... please make sure that people are aware of this. Make sure that nobody attacks him or the people with him."

"Sylas?" she questions, her brows dipping together. "Who the heck is that?"

"That guy I showed up with earlier," I answer. "Aiden's brother."

"Oh." She seems hesitant, but then gives in and nods. "All right, I'll see what I can do... but what are you going to do?"

"I need to find Mathew." I let go of her sleeve and fetch my knife out of my pocket as vampire cries grow louder around the colony.

"I think he went back to his lab." She nods at the building to the side of me.

"Thanks." I spin around and jog back down the street, hoping that Mathew will be there. And that I can find out why Maci wants me to talk to him; protect him. Why it has to be me?

There are no longer guards posted in front of the doorway. Everyone in town has been put on high alert and many of them have stepped up to the wall built out of cars that surrounds the colony. In fact, the wall of broken-down vehicles looks more like a wall of people as they line the top. I wonder how long they'll have to wait there. How long it'll be until the abominations will show up. Maybe we'll end up getting lucky and they won't show up at all. I doubt it, though, and I know that thinking that way can be dangerous.

It's eerily quiet when I open the door and step inside the building where I make my way down the dusty hallway with my knife poised out in front of me; always ready, always on guard, focusing one step ahead, focusing on fighting. I have to be. I don't know when anything's going to show up.

I hear some movement and rustling towards the back of the hallway, and as I get closer, I see Mathew through the doorway to his lab. He's wearing a white coat and is holding some vials filled with various colors of liquid, carefully measuring as he pours each one into a large, silver flask.

He glances up from the flask startled as I enter, a concerned look across his face. At the same time that he ends up spilling a drop or two of the liquid onto the silver table in front of him.

"Is everything okay?" he asks, setting the empty vials down, his fingers trembling. "Have the Highers' army arrived already?"

"Not yet." I cross the room and glance at the jars on the counter filled with an array of liquids. *I wonder what is in them.* "Sylas went to get the other Day Takers to help us." I wonder if I should tell him about Maci and her gift. "And Nichelle's setting up around town, but honestly it could be days before the Highers' army shows up. Or even weeks, depending on how hard it is for the Highers to reach a decision."

He sets the flask down onto the table beside the vials. "Well, at least we'll be ready for them when they get here. And Nichelle is a very good fighter... I'd trust her completely with my life, but she isn't you, Kayla. I'd feel better if you were the one in charge of the others."

"That isn't what I'm supposed to do be doing." It sort of slips out of me and there's no taking it back.

"What do you mean by that?" he wonders, resting his weight against the table, his skin dripping with sweat.

I dither, deciding if I should tell him about Maci. He seems trustworthy, yet at the same time, a lot of people do.

Then again, Maci said I should talk to him. "Maci told me that I'm supposed to protect you and that I need to talk to you about why I do."

"Why would Maci tell you that?" he asks.

"Because…" I sit up on the countertop, letting my legs hang over the edge of the corner, and put my knife in my lap. "She can see things before they happen… she told me that I was going to save the world."

Mathew crosses his arms and his pale eyes flood with curiosity. "I wonder if that was from the experiments?"

"She wasn't just born that way?"

He shakes his head. "Humans weren't born with extraordinary gifts, which are why the Highers were so determined to create them."

I'm not sure if I believe him or not, though, considering he used to be one of the doctors and the cause for all this messing around with humanity. Maybe it was that thought process—that humans had no gifts—that helped their strive to perfection escalate.

He scratches his head. "Did Maci by chance tell you how to save the world? Or how to find the cure even?" he asks, hopeful. It makes me have less hope that he'll be able to find a cure.

His expression sinks as I shake my head. "She didn't tell me how to save it... she never gives instructions, just tidbits of information that will lead me to do the right thing. And she told me that I needed to protect you," I tell him.

He sighs and turns back to the vials on the table. "Yeah, I guess things can't ever be that easy."

"No, they really can't," I agree, reflecting on my difficult past and everything I've gone through to get to this exact point. "But what about you?" I ask. "Did you figure out anything at all yet?"

His pales eyes light up as he picks up a glass vial and holds it up to the light. There is a purple liquid inside the vial that reflects through the glass. "Not yet." He lowers the vial. "But in the papers Aiden left behind, Monarch made several references to how you seemed not to be immune to the original virus in the beginning... that your body reacted to the virus just like everyone else, which means that somewhere along the lines, that changed; you became immune." He places the vial back down on the counter. "So I think the answers might start with you."

I already knew that. I hop off the counter and walk over to him. "So, wait a minute. Are saying that he purposefully injected me with the virus to see if I would turn into a vampire? And then what? I'd turn? How the hell did he change me back?"

"That's the answer we need." He gives me a sympathetic look. "I'm sorry, Kayla. He was determined to find a way to create perfection and he didn't care about those he was hurting. Or killing." He pauses. "He did try to make up for it—tried to reverse the damage he'd done." Mathew starts organizing the vials in rows.

I'm burning in my own anger. Monarch had changed me into a vampire at one point. I was once one of those disgusting monsters crying out at night; hungry and looking to eat flesh and blood. Just like Sylas before he changed.

I swallow my emotions down because I know that I have to—or maybe it's how I've been programmed. "Mathew, there's something I have to tell you." I watch as he sorts through vials, reading the label on them. I hope that I can trust him. "Something important."

He glances up at me with a concerned look on his face. "Kayla, what is it… you look a little ill."

I touch my cheek to my hand, wondering what ill looks like on me. "I feel fine, except I need to tell you something… I just need to know that I can trust you."

He nods, standing up as straight as his crooked back will allow him to. "You can trust me with your life. I promise."

I absorb his truth, feeling a little better. "Back when I went to get the papers and Sylas was there... well, he wasn't there as himself but a... but an abomination..."

He holds up his hands. "Wait, Sylas was an abomination?"

I reluctantly nod. "He was, but then he bit me and well..." I trail off as Mathew's eyes widen.

"Why didn't you tell me this before?" he asks in disbelief, dropping the vial he's holding onto the floor. It shatters at our feet and scatters into fragments around us.

"Because... I wasn't sure I could trust you," I say. It's my initial instinct to mistrust, to keep things to myself, to put walls up. "And besides, it doesn't make any sense. He didn't turn back into a human... he turned back into a Day Taker. Plus, he's bit me before and it didn't do anything at all to him; just made me pass out."

Mathew deliberates what I've said, fiddling with the button on his coat. "What were you when he bit you the first time?"

I shrug. "Whatever you want to consider me before I was a Day Walker," I say. "A soldier... I'm not sure."

"But you were a Day Walker when he bit you the second time?"

I nod, the wheels in my head turning. "Do you think that's what did it? Do you think my Day Walker blood has something to do with the cure?"

His eyes are as wide as I've ever seen before, and without even answering, he whisks over to a cabinet door, his excitement giving him a boost of energy. He opens the door and takes out a syringe. There's a stool next to him and he pats it for me to sit down.

"Why?"

He pauses, uncertain. "If it's all right with you, I'd like to draw some of your blood and study it."

I pull out the stool and sit down on it. "You think studying it will help you figure out a cure?"

"We're about to find out." He pulls the cap off the syringe. "Roll up your sleeve," he instructs. I sigh, but obey, rolling up my sleeve. He presses the needle into my skin, into a vein. It pinches and I watch as the syringe fills up with my blood. When the syringe is full, he removes the needle.

"So now what?" I ask. "How do you study blood?"

He points at this strange looking object over on the counter with a tube attached to it that angles to a platform. "You study blood through that," he says, rolling up his sleeve. "But that's not what I'm doing."

Before I have time to think, he aims the needle at his forearm and plunges it into his vein. My eyes widen as I leap from the stool and reach out to stop him. "You don't know if that is safe!" I exclaim, my fingers snagging the rolled up sleeve of his jacket.

He turns out of my reach and nudges my hand away with his elbow. If I wanted to, I could take him out, but it wouldn't do any good. He's already put some of my blood into his veins.

"What if it doesn't work on you?" I say, stepping back and shaking my head. "What if it only worked on Sylas because he was a Day Taker? Or what if it turns you into a Day Taker or an abomination? There are so many possibilities, Mathew."

"I know that, but that's how all of this started. Risks where taken. Lives were sacrificed." He continues injecting himself with my blood. "Whatever happens doesn't matter… I can either do this or turn or die. I have to try something else."

Sacrifices need to be made. You must understand that, Kayla.

Shaking my head, I sit back down on the stool. "Well, I'm killing you if you turn."

He glances up at me with a ghost smile. "Fair enough."

It grows silent as he takes the needle out of his skin then sets it down on the countertop. I hold my knife and keep my eyes locked on him, ready to slice his chest open if I have to.

He pumps his fist a few times, staring at his arm, waiting for something to happen, I guess.

After some time goes by, I ask, "What do we do now?"

"Now," he says simply, "we wait to see if I turn human or if you have to kill me."

Chapter 21

And we do wait, for a very long time—hours maybe—although I'm not exactly sure since I never did figure out the exact concept of time. Nothing seems to be happening. We make it all the way through the night when Nichelle comes by to inform us that a few vampires tried to break through the wall, but were easily fended off. That ends up being the most excitement we get for the night.

She gave me a weird look when she came into the lab, probably wondering why I was sitting there with Mathew instead of being out with her as well as the others, fighting off vampires. However, neither Mathew nor I offered her any explanation, so she got irritated and left us alone.

"Thanks for not saying anything to her," Mathew tells me after she leaves, slumping down onto the table. He looks exhausted and a little bit weaker than he did before.

"No problem," I respond calmly, yet on the inside I'm worried about how he looks. I'm kicked back on the stool with my legs up on the counter, my back leaning against the wall so I'm facing the door with my knife on my lap. I look relaxed, however I'm anything but. "I didn't think you'd want her worrying about you."

He nods his head, his eyelids fluttering like he's fighting off sleep. "She's very important to me," he says with a yawn. "I hate that she's even out there fighting." His head suddenly begins to wobble around so his forehead is angled and pressed against the surface of the table. Then he shuts his eyes and becomes silent.

I sit up and lower my feet to the ground, wondering if something's happening. My senses go on high alert, my fingers wrap around my knife as I get to my feet. I listen and realize I can no longer hear his heartbeat, so I hurry to his side.

"Mathew, are you okay?" I place my hand on his shoulder and gently shake him, keeping my other arm out to my side, ready to swing it around and stab him in the chest if he sits up and his eyes start bleeding. He limply moves around as I shake him. "Mathew!" I still can't hear his heart beating so I lean over and put my ear beside his face, trying to hear if he's breathing. All I hear is silence and I feel no breath.

Jesus, did it kill him?

I pull my hand away and turn for the door to get help, hoping someone else around here can understand medical stuff enough to know what's going on. I'm halfway there when I hear it. Soft at first, but then it increases; rapid, loud and sturdy.

Thump… Thump… Thump… Thump…

I quickly spin around and race back to the table as Mathew elevates his head and focuses on me, blinking his eyes as he looks around in disbelief. I put my hand in front of me, the sharp tip of the knife angled at his throat, but then he opens his eyes widely; my knife slips from my hand and hits the floor.

His eyes are no longer pale. They're green, like how grass used to look.

"Holy shit," I say, stunned.

He lets out a shaky breath as he sits up straighter. "What's wrong?" He looks at me worriedly. "Did it work?"

"I'm not sure… but…" I scoop up my knife and inch closer to him, "but your eyes are green… and your skin looks less pale."

Mathew's green eyes widen as he touches his finger-tips to the bottom of his eyes. Then he examines his skin over, putting his arms out in front of him, turning them over, noting that it looks healthy and smooth. When he looks at me, he's in a state of awe.

"I feel so much better," he says and even his voice sounds stronger.

I open my mouth to ask if he thinks it worked—if maybe that's the cure—or if he thinks he might have turned into a Day Taker—or worse something else—but we're interrupted when Nichelle bursts inside the room, panting and gasping for air. Mathew purposefully looks in the other direction from her, as though he's working on something at the table.

"Sylas is back with the others," she says, breathless, pressing her hand to her chest as she reaches the center of the room.

"That's good." Mathew pretends to be moving things around. "Why don't you send him in here? But just him, not the others."

She nods, giving his back an inquisitive look. "Are you okay?"

"I'm fine." He shoos her away. "Just really busy."

She still looks lost as she turns and exits the room, letting the door bang shut behind her.

"Why are you hiding from her?" I ask him, sitting down at the table beside him.

He glances up at me, looking even healthier than he did before Nichelle ran in. "I don't want to get anyone's hopes up yet. Not until we can be sure I'm cured. For all I know, my blood still might not be human. And if it does work, we need to find a way to make it in large amounts—enough to cure everyone that has been infected... because it's going to take more blood than you have in your body."

I glance down at the veins in my arms, purple just below my pale skin. "Do you have any idea on how to do that? How to tell what you are and how to create my blood?"

He shakes his head. "I'm not sure, but I'm going to start by studying your blood and mine. And..." He trails off as he wanders over to the counter, his strides so much sturdier, and he carries his back straighter.

He bends down in front of one of the bottom cabinets and then glances over his shoulder before slipping his hand into his pocket. He takes out a key and moves it towards a lock on the cabinet door.

"What are you doing?" I ask as he unlocks the door.

He drops the key into his pocket, opens the door up and then reaches inside. "Getting something important." When he pulls back and stands up, he has a vial in his hand.

"What's that in your hand?" I question, gripping the handle of my knife while wondering if he's up to something; if maybe he's turning into a Higher. His hair isn't white, though, or his eyes. Plus, he has emotion in his expression.

He slowly lowers his gaze to the vial in his hand as he unfolds his fingers from the glass. Then stretches his arm out to me. "This is the original virus."

I step back, stunned. "What?"

"The original vampire virus," he says. "This is what started it all."

It doesn't look like something that would harm the world; in fact, it looks innocent. White and sparkly. When the liquid hits the light, it shines brighter than anything I've ever seen.

"That's it?" I ask, leaning in to get a good look at it. "That's what changed the world to what it is?"

He shakes his head as he tucks the virus into his pocket. "No, a lot of greed was the cause of why the world is what it is," he says. "But yes, this is what started the vampire spread." He pauses as he gets lost in thought. "It spread so quickly, you know. One host would get infected and feed off something then who they fed off would change and start to feed. Within days, well, the world was a mess. The Highers took the opportunity to make it seem like they could offer protection when really what they wanted was control and more test subjects to use to find their perfection."

I frown, remembering the colony. "I can remember."

He smiles sadly. "You can remember what the world is, but not what the world was. It wasn't that bad of a place."

I wish I could remember it all, but I only have bits and pieces of my memories. I wonder if they'll all come back to me. "So why do you have that?"

"Well, I kept it mainly to study it and try to figure out a way to get rid of it," he says, closing his fingers around it. "But now I'm going to study it to figure out how it replicates itself. How it takes over the body of the host and turns them into a virus."

"Why, though?" I ask. "Shouldn't you be studying yourself and seeing if you're human."

"I am," he says, placing the virus carefully into his pocket. "But I want to study this, too. If we did find the cure and it's in your blood, the virus might help us figure out a way to spread it quickly. If we can figure out the process, then we can replicate it with the cure."

"So that every person infected with the cure becomes the cure," I say, nodding understandingly.

"Yes," he says brightly as he whisks over to the table. "Now I just have to see if you and I are the answers to the cure."

"Why would you two be the answer to the cure?" Sylas says from behind me.

Mathew's green eyes widen and he quickly tries to turn away before Sylas can see he's healing. Sylas strides over to him, grabs his shoulder and with a lot of effort, forces Mathew to turn around to face him. He observes him closely; the once weak man who now looks a lot younger, stronger and has green eyes that were once pale.

"Did you do it? Did you find a cure?" he asks Mathew in shock. When Mathew doesn't respond, Sylas looks at me. "Kayla, what's going on?"

"We might have found something," I say. "But…" Before I can further explain, Sylas moves up to me and throws his arms around me in the weirdest embrace ever. "I can't believe it," he says, pulling me closer to him. "We have a cure. Finally, we have something to fight for."

He seems so much more weightless, like his rough shell has crumbled with the idea that there's hope. More than I would have expected and part of me wonders if his whole tough guy act was a facade created to mask the worry that we'd never protect or save the world. I'm about to tell him that we might not have a cure—that Mathew isn't even sure if he's human, and if he is, we're not even sure how to make enough of a cure to spread it yet—but he seems so happy, and Sylas never seems happy, so I decide to follow what Mathew did and keep quiet. Mathew and I exchange a look and make a silent agreement to keep our lips sealed.

"So what do we do now?" Sylas asks, pulling away. His dark eyes look brighter and his expression not so hard.

He has a smudge of dirt on his cheek and I rub it off with my thumb. "We fight."

Sylas nods with enthusiasm. "That, I can do."

"Good." I force a smile, feeling my own lie all over me, but shake it off and go forward, trying to be the fearless leader everyone seems to expect me to be. "Can you do me a favor? Can you go check on Maci for me and make sure her and Greyson are safe? After that, find Nichelle. Make sure that the Day Takers and her people are cooperating... I'm a little worried about certain personalities conflicting"

"Since when do you get to say the orders?" Sylas questions with a teasing arch of his brow.

"Since you started asking me questions," I reply in a joking tone, but I'm being serious.

He assesses me over with a look that used to make me nervous, although it sort of makes me excited now. Then he nods, putting his hand on my hip, fingers delving into my skin. I jump, shocked by the intimate touch as he slowly slides up to my side. His fingers dip into my skin roughly, but I barely feel a sting. Then he pulls me towards him and I resist for a moment before letting him guide my lips. He kisses deeply, exploring my mouth with his tongue until Monarch clears his throat and we break away.

"I'll be back as soon as I check on things," he says with a wink before turning around and heading out the door.

I blow out a breath and then sink onto the floor and drop my face into my hands. "I don't like lying very much."

"No one does," Mathew says as he begins sorting through his cabinets.

I take a few deep breaths then compose myself before raising my head up. "So now what?"

"Now, I study." He frowns. "But I just hope I have enough time... I hate to think it, but if I don't get this all figured out before the Highers and their army show up here, then they'll likely destroy everything, including my lab. At that point, all hope will be lost."

"First off, we don't know when they're going to show up," I say. "And if they do, we—I won't let them ruin the lab."

He doesn't seem convinced and I get up from my chair and stride towards the door, pausing to look back at Mathew. "Work on figuring it out. I'll make sure nothing gets in or out of here."

He swallows hard and then nods, but I can tell he doesn't think I can do it. However, I have to, no matter what. "Kayla, wait," he calls out before I step out.

I pause, turning around. "Yeah."

"Would it be all right if I drew some more of your blood?" he asks. "To study and for…" He rubs his neck tensely. "Just in case something happens to you, I'll still have something to study."

"Oh, of course." I return to him and hop up onto the table, rolling up my sleeve as he grabs another syringe. "But Mathew, as far as I know, I don't… well, I haven't figured out a way that anything could happen to me."

"You don't think you can die?"

I shrug. "As far as I can tell, no. It makes me wonder if the cures living inside me if… if I can ever be human again." I'm not sure how I feel about this revelation, if I like the idea that I'll always be different. Honestly, I don't think I do. How can we ever change back the world if I stay the same; if I'm always there to study and replicate, like the Highers want to?

He offers me a smile. "Maybe your right… maybe Monarch did create perfection in you, but then again, if I've learned anything, it's that everything has a weakness."

***

After I'm finished giving Mathew some of my blood, I walk out of the building. It's quiet for the most part. Most of the people have barricaded themselves inside the buildings and homes while the rest stand their posts at the wall. Just a ways to my right, Nichelle is standing by the wall, noticing me as I make my way down to the street.

"Kayla," she calls out, heading over to me with a torch in her hand. She has a thick leather belt strapped around her waist and a sword secured in it. "What were you doing in there with Mathew? And why was he so sketchy?"

"I…" I trail off as I see them moving towards me.

A row of different collections, people who carry different powers, yet share the same genetics for the most part. They stand out like a sore thumb; dark clothes, leather, their hair colors like fire and ash. Their skin is smooth, features flawless and the sounds of their hearts are still.

Sylas stands in the middle and uses his long legs to stride over to me. He has an arrogant look on his face, but it vanishes when he reads my face like an open book. "What's wrong with you… you look upset."

"There's nothing wrong," I reply, pulling myself together.

"Is it about the cure?" he asks, folding his arms.

Nichelle's head whips in his direction. "Cure?"

219

"Yeah..." Sylas's eyes stay on me and I wonder if he can sense my uneasiness. "They found a cure... maybe."

A big grin spreads across Nichelle's face. "Yes!!" she exclaims, throwing her hands in the air. "I knew Mathew would figure it out. God, it's so great! We finally have some good news!"

"You're making a lot of noise," I tell her as people start glancing in our direction. She settles down a little, but still has way too much energy. "Mathew thinks he might have found a cure, but there's still a lot of other stuff to figure out," I say, and their moods deflate a notch. "What we need to make sure of is that he's protected at all times. Nichelle, I need you to put a lot of guards around his lab and make sure they're there always... it's important that he can keep working no matter what happens... and that him and his lab are safe."

She nods and turns around, jogging off towards a solider-looking group of people who aren't nearly as strong as the Day Takers, but probably as close as you can get in human form. She says something to them and then they head over towards the lab with swords and knives in their hands. I wonder if it's enough; if they'll be able to stop the abominations from getting in if they do show up. I wonder if Mathew will figure it out in time. I wonder a lot of things at that moment and all the answers make me feel... well, hopeless. The feeling sucks.

I glance over at the Day Takers who are just standing there, watching me. All six of them. I don't know any of them except for one; a tall girl with red hair, wearing a long, flowing skirt and who has the powers to dip into people's heads.

"Emmy," I say cautiously, remembering how she's slightly off her rocker. "Can you come here for a minute? I need to ask you a favor."

Her deep red lips spread into a smile and then she struts forward, swishing her skirt.

"Do you really want to go there?" Sylas questions amusedly. "You know how she can get."

"Yeah, but I need her to help protect the lab," I say to Sylas. "Mathew... he's the one who can figure all this out."

"But it's your blood?" he states. "We should be protecting you, too."

"Mathew has some of my blood just in case something happens to me," I reply. "Besides, I don't think anything can. I've died plenty of times and I always heal."

"You say that like it's a bad thing."

"No, I say it like it's a thing that'll be a problem in the future if things do go back to the way that they should be."

He opens his mouth to say something with a strange look on his face, but Emmy interrupts us, stepping unnecessarily close to me.

"Well, well," she says. "If it isn't the beautiful Kayla." She taps her finger on her lips and then breathes in my scent. "Looking for me to dip into your head again." She strokes my hair with her fingers and Sylas chuckles from behind her.

"Actually, no." I step back out of her reach. "I just need you and two other Day Takers to go help guard that building over there." I point over my shoulder at the lab.

She frowns. "You want me to help protect a building; one that humans are already protecting?"

"Please," I say. "It's really important."

She crosses her arms and stares me down. "And what do I get out of this."

Sylas nudges her in the back, a little rough. "Emmy, stop being a pain in the ass and go."

She huffs and stomps her foot. "God, this is so ridiculous," she whines, but ends up obeying, going over and getting two other Day Takers to come with her. One of them is really tall and muscular while the other is shorter, though equally as strong in appearance. When they walk by us, they all give me a dirty look.

"Glad to see they still feel the same way about me," I say, tracking them with my gaze until they arrive at the lab.

I return my attention to Sylas when he brushes the inside of my wrist with his fingers before taking my hand. "Come with me for a bit," he says. "I need to talk to you about something."

"What's wrong?" I ask as he starts to pull me down the path.

He doesn't speak as we head deeper into the shadows of the town and farther out of the eyes of Day Takers and humans. He only lets go of my hand when we arrive at a section where the ground bowls inward and all that's around us are hills and the wall of cars.

"What about Aiden?" he asks as he releases my fingers from his hold and steps back to look at me.

"What about him?" I ask, glancing around, wondering why he brought me down here.

He considers something and then starts to circle around me with his hands behind his back. "All this talk about protecting everyone in here, especially Mathew, but what happens if Aiden shows up here with them, too?"

Through all the chaos, this detail had sort of slipped my mind and the only solution pains me. Yet, saving the world is the most important thing at this point.

"We'll have to stop him," I say quietly. "If he gets in the way."

"Can you do that?" he questions, stopping in front of me, inspecting my reaction closely.

I swallow hard and nod. "I can if I have to." I pause, gathering my voice. "Can you?"

His eyes hold mine, like he's pretending it's no big deal, but I can see in his eyes that it is. "I'll stop him if he gets in the way."

We grow quiet and eventually he turns to stare at the wall with his hands stuffed in his pocket. We can hear the sounds of voices drifting down to us as the people in town and on the walls talk way too loud.

"You know, they make a lot of noise for someone who's in trouble," he remarks, looking at me again; his dark eyes look even blacker, like coal.

"They're human," I say. "They don't know anything else."

"You think they can handle this?" he wonders with zero confidence. "If they can fight against the abominations and stand a chance?"

I shrug, being honest. "I'm not sure... Maci seems to think I can do something about all this... protect everyone, or at least Mathew." I sit down on the ground in the dirt and he joins me. "But at the same time, I'm just one tiny person going up against a herd of large, vicious monsters. Yeah, I can't die or become infected, but I also can't make sure *everyone* else doesn't either."

He sits down beside me and bumps his shoulder into mine. "I wasn't asking if you can handle it... I know you can." He leans back on his hands and we stare at the hillside. "I was asking if you think they can handle it." He nods his head at a group of humans standing just above us on the wall.

I want to say yes, but deep down I know that'd be a lie. "I honestly don't know," I say. "But I guess we'll have to hope for the best."

"You're basing a lot of this on hope." He leans into me, wetting his lips with his tongue. "But you're forgetting one thing."

"And what's that?" I glance at his lips as he gets closer.

He pauses just as his lips almost connect with mine. "That you're the perfect soldier." Then he kisses me and I want to pull back as I tell him he's wrong. That I'm flawed. That I can't die. Can't change. That I'm pretty much motionless.

Instead, I keep kissing him because, for a moment, it makes everything easier.

Chapter 22

Sylas and I continue to sneak off and kiss for the next few days, trying to distract our minds from what we face ahead. I check on Mathew, make walk-throughs around the town and generally check on everything. With each day I start to wonder if something has happened; if maybe Aiden didn't make it to them or if the Highers couldn't agree to send out the army. Deep down, though, I know that's not true. They'll come. They always do.

People have started to let their guard down by staying out later or not keeping such a close eye on the desert land when the sun goes down. Some even bail out and head for the hills; not wanting to protect their town, but hide. It's driving me mad, but there's nothing I can do. They won't listen to me because I'm not human; something which I try not to think about.

On the fourth day, when I stop by to check up on Mathew, I decide to talk to him about it; to see if he'll talk to them about being more careful.

"You need to talk to your people," I announce as I enter his lab. "They're..." I trail off at the sight of the mess that surrounds him. Empty vials are strewn everywhere, flasks, garbage, spilt liquids on the floor, and Mathew stands in it all with his eyes pressed to that strange device he pointed at the other day; the one he said would help him study our blood.

"What on earth," I say, maneuvering around the mess. "Don't you ever clean up in here?"

He falters back with his hand pressed to his heart, his elbow bumping the counter and putting a dent in it. *Strange.* "Goodness, I didn't hear you come in."

"I said something as I walked in," I say, glass crunching under my boot, eyeing over his extremely healthy state. I mean, he's been looking healthier and healthier by the day, but he's almost glowing with strength. "Didn't you hear me?"

He shakes his head, looking distracted. "No... no... I was..." He drifts off as he puts his eyes back on the strange device, turning the knob on the side. "Well, I was having an epiphany."

"Over what?"

He glances up at me, his eyes shining with excitement. "Over a cure."

I rush up to him. "You figured it out?"

"Well, yes and no." He gestures at himself as he squares his shoulders. "I've been studying my blood and well..." he trails off, glancing around with a puzzled look. Then something clicks in his expression and he hurries back to the wall.

"What are you...?"

I trail off as he rams his fist through the wall. Bits and pieces of brick shatter and fly through the air. My jaw hits my knees as I gape at him, stepping back as my hand moves to my knife.

"What are you?" I ask, drawing my knife out of my back pocket.

He surrenders his hands in front of him. "Kayla, relax. I'm still me, simply stronger... just like you."

My arm falls to my side. "Are you saying what I think you're saying?"

He lowers his hands and rushes towards me, beaming from ear to ear. "Yes," he says. "You're blood didn't just cure me; it turned me into a Day Walker."

"That can't be possible," I argue against the bluntly honest truth in front of me. I can see it in his eyes; the power, the strength, the confidence. "Sylas didn't..." I trail off, remembering how he seemed to be stronger as we ran here and how, when he kisses me, there is so much more behind it I thought I'd bruise. I've never felt like I could bruise before. Unlike Mathew, however, I'm not happy. "Well, that doesn't do us any good," I say. "Because we're not trying to turn the world into a bunch of Day Walkers. We want to be human again, right?"

"Of course," he says and I can tell he means it, that he wants the world to return to what it was. "And we're one step closer to it."

"How so?"

"Because..." He hurries over to the cabinet, unintentionally smashing things in as he goes. "Now I understand the way the virus and the cure work." He takes out a few vials and the leftover papers of Monarchs with his handwriting scribbled all over them. "Monarch kept rambling in these," he says, staring down at the papers. "How he managed to make you immune to the vampire virus even before you were changed into..." He peeks over at me with an apologetic face. "Well, before he turned you into whatever you were before you were a Day Walker." He taps his finger on the papers. "It means at one point you were still in human form and withstanding the virus." He gathers the papers and vials and then moves over to the table, arranging them out.

"When I was injected with your blood, my blood took on the structure of yours," he says. "Therefore, I became a Day Walker, so if I can return you to your human state, then your blood could turn any person back to their human state."

"But wouldn't you be making a cure by turning me back into a human?"

He shakes his head. "There's something in your blood, Kayla; something that kills the virus instantly. So if we can break down the various viruses in you and eliminate them, then we might be able to get you back to your human form," he says. "It would make you a viable host and cure because your blood would not only heal the infected person and change them back to human, but it would also protect them when getting bit again."

"But what if when you turn me back," I say. "Then I'm no longer the cure; what if it's my Day Walker blood that's the cure."

He shakes his head. "I already told you, Monarch said you weren't responding to the virus even when you were a child," he says. "But honestly I don't know, not until we try it."

"But what if you try it and then I change back and I'm merely useless."

"I'm not going to lie to you, Kayla. It's a risk. You just need to decide if you want to take it. And I'd make sure to have a lot of your original blood on hand as backup."

I'm not sure how to respond. He acts like he's playing mad scientist, which is what started this entire problem in the first place. So many things could go wrong. "And how would you even do it?" I ask. "Figure out how to turn me back to human?"

He swallows hard, his cheery demeanor darkening a little. "There was this thing we used to do called a fading," he says. "Back in my experiment days, after a subject had been tested and tested on, we'd try to wipe the virus out of their bodies so we could start the testing process on them again; make them usable again, like a clean slate."

I give him a dirty look. "And did they live?"

He bites on his lip, looking guilty. "Most didn't, but a few strong ones did," he says.

"And what were they like?" I say coldly. "These people that you *faded*. Were they normal humans again?"

He runs his fingers through his hair then reclines back against the table. "I'd try to lie to you, but from what I understand from Monarchs notes about you, he made it so you could tell when someone is lying." He releases a stressed breath. "So the answer is yes, they were human, but no they weren't the same. They lost a lot of their function, although their bodies still thrived."

I step forward in a threatening manner, wondering if I can take him now or if his strength will match mine. I'm curious to find out. "So what you're saying is that if I take this fading, then there's a good chance I'll be gone."

He wavers then gets to his feet and walks over to me. "Gone, but for the greater good. I'm sorry I have to say this, but sometimes it takes a huge sacrifice to make things right again. Not everyone can survive."

His words almost match Monarchs words; the ones I constantly hear in my head. Is that what he's trying to tell me? That this is the sacrifice."

"I have to think about it," I say then turn for the door.

"Kayla, wait," he calls out. "I need one more thing from you."

Shaking my head, I turn around. "What?"

He looks taken aback by my anger, but shrugs it off. "I need to inject you with the original vampire virus."

"Why?" I gape at him.

"Because I need to see if I can get your blood to replicate like the virus does. And I want to start by seeing what will happen if I add it to your blood."

"But I've already been bit. Nothing happens."

He shakes his head, his expression laced with stress. "The virus itself works a lot different... and it's more potent when you shoot it straight into a vein."

"So you're saying I could turn?" God, what does this man want from me? First he's asking me to risk my existence and give over my body for the hope of mankind and now he's asking me to take a risk and turn into a vampire.

"I doubt it," he says. "I just wanted to let you know that it's a risk because I don't want to lie to you."

"Can't lie to me," I remind him, annoyed. I consider it for a moment, wondering what the right choice is. I could turn into one. Let my flesh rot. Do I want that for myself? Then I remember that there are risks that need to be taken in order for things to change and then decide to do it. "You have some of my blood, right?" I ask, sitting down on a chair. "As backup, so you can hopefully change me back with it?"

He nods, pointing at a row of vials in the cabinet. "I do and any signs that you're changing, I'll inject you."

I shove my sleeve up. "Then do it. Go ahead and inject me."

He seems remorseful, but still goes to retrieve the vial from his cabinet. He fills a syringe with it then flicks the needle with his fingertip as he makes his way back over to me. A slow breath eases from his lips as he aims it at my arm and I frown as he runs his finger along my vein, remembering, yet not remembering, all the times I was injected. Then, with a deep breath, he injects the virus straight into me and all we can do is wait.

***

"I feel funny," I say, feeling a little woozy as he throws away the syringe and returns the virus to its rightful place in the cabinet.

"That's understandable." He turns around, watching me, waiting to see if I'll change.

I brace myself against the wall as the room starts to spin; my veins feel like they're on fire. "I feel like I'm going to throw up."

Nodding and keeping his eyes fastened on me, he backs away to a metallic cooler in the corner of the room. He opens it up and takes out a small vial of my blood along with another vial that looks like it's filled with a black liquid that bubbles red. He tucks that one into his pocket and then hurries forward, preparing to inject me with my blood.

I hold up my finger, struggling to breathe, not ready to give up. I force my body to fight against the potency and desire to let the virus take control. After a few inhales and exhales, my strength returns to me and I manage to stand up straight, releasing a breath.

"I think I'm going to be okay," I tell him, squaring my shoulders.

"You don't feel like your skin is peeling off or anything?" he asks cautiously. "Or are you filled with a hunger for blood?"

I shake my head, breathing freer and freer by the second. "I feel perfectly fine."

His whole body sinks as he sighs with relief. "Thank God." He moves over to a drawer and gets an empty vial and syringe. "I'm going to take some of your blood now and see what it's doing. Have a seat."

I do what he says as he prepares to draw my blood. I eye his pocket, wondering what the other vial is. "What was that other thing you grabbed?" I ask.

He touches his finger to my forearm, finding a vein. "What do you mean?"

"That vial that's in your pocket. What is it?"

He puts the needle into my arm and begins to fill the syringe up with blood. "That's the fading."

I don't say anything as he finishes up and then I get up from my chair, heading to leave.

"Wait, where are you going?" he asks as I reach the doorway.

I pause. "To think."

Now, he pauses. "Kayla, I know this is a hard decision but—but we're running out of time."

"I know that," I say through gritted teeth. "But I need just a few minutes." To think. To process. To find out what Sylas thinks."

I walk out the door, knowing if Mathew wanted to, he could probably chase me down and try to put the fading in me, but he doesn't. He's giving me a choice. When I think about it, though, I know it's really not a choice. Deep down, I know what I'm going to do because it's why I was created. To think without emotion, to think about what's important, to not base my decisions on greed.

In the end, I'll go through with it. I just need to say good-bye.

Chapter 23

The first thing I do is find Sylas. Then I tell him everything I found out, including that he might be a Day Walker now. We do a few tests and determine that he probably is, which seems to excite him. I just hope the power doesn't go to his head, like it did with Aiden.

Then we move onto the bigger problem. The fading. I'm nervously pacing a section of the wall, telling myself it's time to say good-bye, move forward and hope for the best, however it's hard. I'm conflicted and I don't like it because it's for selfish reasons and I don't want to be selfish like the Highers.

"How can we be sure we can trust him?" Sylas asks. He's leaning against the wall with one of his knees pulled up and his arm resting on it.

I shrug as I continue to pace. "I know he's not lying, but at the same time, I know that he knows it might not work and I might just end up becoming a useful body in the end."

He rubs his eyes as he stares at the ground. "So then, is it worth it?" he asks. "To do that to yourself when you're so perfect right now."

I stop walking and try to stay neutral. "Sylas, perfection is what got the world in trouble to begin with." I gesture around at the town hidden behind a wall of cars as vampires cry out on the other side. "None of this would be here. If it wasn't for perfection, you and I'd be…"

He glances up at me, his dark eyes filled with heat. "We'd be what?"

I shrug. "I don't know… walking around and living our lives… normal."

His brow arches. "Together."

I press my lips together and shrug again. "I'm not sure. Maybe."

He slowly gets to his feet, his eyes glued to mine as he inches towards me, reducing the space between our bodies until we're nearly flush. "And if we were together in a normal world, what would we be doing?"

"I've never really thought about it," I say. "Because I can barely remember what the real world was like."

"Hmmm..." He considers something thoughtfully. "Would we be doing this?" He leans in and brushes his lips against mine, tasting me softly.

"Maybe," I whisper against his lips and then he kisses me again, much deeper. His hands slip around my waist, forcing me closer, pressing us together. I don't fight it because I want it; want to be close to him for a moment. We kiss until it becomes too hot, too intense, too emotional, then we pull back. His eyes are still shut and he touches his lips with his fingers.

"Kayla, I'm not going to tell you what to do," he says. "No, I don't want you to do it, but at the same time, I don't think you could live with yourself if you didn't do it." His eyes open. "You have too good of a heart."

I put my hand over my hollow chest. "It doesn't even beat anymore."

He places his hand over mine. "It's still in there though, and it's full of good."

I'm about to open my mouth and tell him the same, even though I know he'll argue, but then we hear a loud thump followed by a scream. Sylas and I trade a look. I think we both know the moment our eyes lock that this is it.

They're here. We can sense it in the air, hear soft thuds in the distance, and the cries of the vampires have faded.

Seconds later, we hear someone yell, "They're coming!"

"Shit," Sylas says, taking off for the wall.

I run after him, my footsteps still quicker and I end up passing him. I scan the top of the wall as I move and then head towards a rounder man holding a weird glasses looking thing to his eyes that supposedly helps humans have vision like vampires, although I'm skeptical.

Sylas is right at my heels as I move effortlessly up the stack of cars, running up pieces sticking out like they're stairs. When I reach the top, I summon a breath and take in the sight before me. Barreling at us at full speed are a large group of abominations, moving on all fours, tearing up the sand and rocks and creating a dust storm as they plow over any vampires in the way. There's more than I expected. Way more. And they move so much quicker out in the open, hilly land then they do in the city streets.

And they're not alone.

Moving beside them are white figures, their robes blowing in the wind along with their snowy white hair. There's also one figure wearing all black that blends in with the night, yet his hair has streaks of white. When I squint closer and examine them closely, I make out Gabrielle and Monarch in the crowd along with... Aiden. He's starting to change into a higher, too, which means he'll be less like himself and more like them.

I start to see the bigger picture at the moment; the things I could change if Mathew can make the fading work. That sweet boy I first met would never have had to go through this; no one would ever have to again.

Sylas must see his brother, too, because he reaches over and takes my hand like he needs to hold onto something. I give it a squeeze since it's all that I can do. I feel a slight twitch of his fingers as his firm jaw tightens.

"I hope we're ready for this," he mutters, letting go of my hand and collecting one of the many sharpened sticks on the top of the wall. "God, there's so many of them."

I slowly nod, taking in the people around us. I hate to think it, but I can't help seeing how easily the abominations could destroy them. They weren't built for this. They're weak and one bite will ruin them. So fragile. So helpless against the virus. Everyone except for me. I stand tall in the crowd, the single thing that could possibly save them.

If I can convince myself to go through with it.

"Well, it looks like we're going to need more people on the wall," Sylas says in a fake joking tone. "God, this is worse than I thought it would be... there's just so many."

I nod, turning around and hating what I see. All the guards and the people of the town have gathered around me on the wall or below the wall, waiting to fight as they look at me with their eyes pleading at me to say something, do something... help them and tell them what to do.

Some of the Day Takers have migrated to them, too, not looking afraid, but entertained. Thankfully, Emmy has managed to keep herself over by the lab so Mathew's protected. Does it even matter? Can he cure the world without me? Do I need to survive? Can I even die?

There's a pause in the chatter below me as they wait for me to tell them what to do. I turn and glance at the stampede heading for us then turn back to the unmoving crowd.

I want to tell them to run.

Run for the lives.

Flee.

I summon a deep breath then slip my fingers out of Sylas's and step forward to the brink of the wall. "The

Highers, the ones who started all this—the virus and the whole crumbling of the world, will be here soon. And they're strong—stronger than the vampires," I tell them. Shocks and gasps follow as they all look around at each other. Their fear instantly gives me a headache. "And the abominations are with them..." I remember they have no idea what abominations are so I add, "They're the things caused by a Highers bite. And these monsters are more animal than human... and they're fast, large, and complicated to fight."

"How many are there?" Nichelle calls out from the crowd below, stepping up to the front.

I glance at Sylas for help, wondering if we should lie— if it would be better if they didn't know how little of a chance they stand against the army. "What should I tell them," I hiss.

He moves forward and his voice booms out over the crowd, "A lot." I cringe against his truth and he shrugs. "They need to know, Kayla, otherwise they won't prepare themselves for the worst."

"We're all going to be killed!" a person to the left of me says, dropping his spear onto the ground. It hits one of the metal cars below us and then suddenly everyone starts to panic.

"We should flee while we can!" a man from below shouts, looking around at the others as he hurries to the back of the crowd, ready to bail. "We should go! Go to the caves or the hills like the others did earlier."

"Even if you did flee, they'll chase you down; the Highers don't just give up," Sylas informs them in a bored tone. "There's too many of them and they are too fast. Run and you'll be killed."

"I'd rather run than sit here and wait for them," someone says and then suddenly everyone is agreeing, nodding their heads and turning to run away.

"Wait," I call out, not knowing what to do. They need something to keep them here. Something to give them motivation. "You have to stay and fight... if not for yourselves then for Mathew... and the cure."

They pause, some turning around. One man, a gangly one with curly brown hair and long limbs, strides forward. "There's a cure?" he asks, pushing his way to the front of the mob.

A woman with jet-black hair says, "Impossible. She's lying."

"I never lie," I say, which is a lie, but it's called for at the moment. "And if you leave, then it'll be gone. So please. Stay. We must protect Mathew and the cure. It could save humanity. Change it back to what it was."

"But what was it?" a lanky man asks, glancing around at the crowd who are all intently listening to him, ready to believe the next thing out of his mouth. "Was it this? Or was it something else? How do we know it'll be better than this?"

I glance over my shoulder at the abominations and Highers getting closer, the cloud of dirt on the outskirts thickening. "Because it has to be."

They chatter amongst each other and then the sounds slowly fade away. When I return my attention to them, most of them are watching me except for a few who are running towards the street, bailing out on the fight.

"For the cure!" one of them shouts out, raising his hand in the air.

The rest shout out the same thing and then people start to climb up the walls with knives and swords in their hands, lining the top of the wall with their bodies. Some have sticks, some have spears like Sylas is carrying. Others just have their hands as their weapon, but it's all we have.

I let out a breath of relief. "God, that was hard. It's like they wanted to listen to whatever anyone was saying at the time"

"That would be human nature." Sylas pats my back. "But you did good convincing them with a cure."

I look up at him. "Yeah, I guess... now I just have to figure out a way to give them a cure if they make it through this."

"I think you already know that will happen," he says sadly.

"You have a lot of confidence in me."

"Because I know you well enough to know you'll do what you believe in, and saving the world is what you believe in."

I wish I had his confidence because he seems so sure and I seem so uncertain.

"Stop worrying," he commands, eyes darken as a slow smile spreads across his face. "How about one last kiss before we die?"

I roll my eyes again, yet then, knowing he's right, knowing that we might not make it through this—that none of us might—I stand up on my tiptoes and kiss him passionately, letting my emotions temporarily take me over as I thread my fingers through his hair. In response, his tongue slips into my mouth and twines with mine. We might have gone for a hell of a lot longer, but then someone screams and we pull away, knowing it's time.

I give Sylas a look that I hope conveys good-bye and he nods his head in a silent understanding. Then, at the same time, we spring to the edge of a wall. He hands me the long, sharpened stick that he's been carrying around and I take it, knowing it's not going to help me that much against the forces before us.

Knowing all this, we still step forward and join the line.

The enormous army of abominations is now less than a hundred feet from the wall and closing in on us fast. The sounds of their footsteps shockwave around us as their feet pound against the ground. Pointing my spear out, I prepare for whatever is to come next while reminding myself what this is for. It's for them, the people standing around me, ready to die, so that maybe, just maybe, the world can change.

I watch them get closer, hearing the rapid acceleration of hearts around me. Thump... thump. Thump, thump, thump.

I hold my breath and wait.

Thump... thump...

The footsteps get closer.

The people around me breathe fiercer.

The footsteps grow louder.

Suddenly, I swear there's a pause where everything in the world freezes.

Then, all at once, the abominations strike into the wall like a raging earthquake. I brace myself for the impact as the entire wall wobbles and shifts with the weight of their enormous bodies. They howl out at the night as several people stumble backwards, screaming as they fall to the ground below, hitting it with a thud. One man falls forward and gets ripped to pieces in seconds by the beasts. Someone starts to cry while the others with spears aim and throw them at the beasts. Several abominations stagger back as the sharp end of the spears pierces into their chest, but it barely puts a dent in the numbers of beasts down below. Seconds later, they start to climb up the wall, bending and ripping the metal to pieces.

People take their knives and swords to stab at the abominations' chests, faces—anything they can reach— screaming and crying out, scared out of their minds. The abominations bite back, fangs snarling, tearing off limps, howling at the knives and peeling off flesh as they shed their own. Humans and abominations start falling to the ground and piling up in numbers, their blood staining the ground below them and creating a river.

One abomination manages to make it onto the wall, right beside me and I whirl around with my leg out and slam my boot into its chest. It growls, staggering with its crooked, warped legs, but doesn't fall. Instead, it dives towards me with its fangs out, clamping its jaw. I swing the spear around as it opens its mouth to devour me and the pointy end spears straight into its mouth and exits out the other side of its jaw. I jerk it out and blood spills over the ground as its knees give out. I kick it to the ground, adding it to the growing pile of bodies.

I'm about to relax when another makes it to my side between Sylas and me. I start to move for it, but stop and watch as Sylas's arm darts out in my direction. Before I can even blink, he has the handle of my spear in his hand and shoves the end into the abominations chin. Then spins around, lifts the spear above his head and jabs it through its skull. We both stick our feet out at the same time and kick it to the ground towards the pile of bodies, both human and beast.

He exchanges a look with me as we breathe in the sight and then his lips part like he's about to say something when someone yells out.

"Over there, towards the East part of the wall!" a man yells, pointing in that direction. "They're starting to be overrun!"

Sylas glances around and then nods his head in that direction. I follow his gaze, my eyes widening at the sight of people fighting off the beasts, launching them back off and slicing them when they get near the top. The abominations just keep coming in huge clusters and the cars that create the wall are starting to buckle below their weight.

One abomination grabs a woman by the leg, sinking his teeth into her then bounds off the wall, taking her with them. They disappear into the group below, a sea of drooling beast, flesh peeling off, rotting, legs crooked, yet they're strong.

Sylas nudges me in the back to go and we take off towards where they're being overtaken, making a path along the top of the wall while keeping our eyes on the section about to collapse.

Another abomination jumps up onto the wall by my side as I'm heading there and pounces on top of me, side swiping me. Its rotting flesh slams against my face as I fall to the ground. I can smell its putrid scent as it covers me with its decaying body. I flip over onto my back and move to put my legs up, but it hovers over me, snarling, and then opens its mouth to take a bite. I manage to get my legs up and kick forcefully upward, launching it off me. Then, I spring to my feet, looking around for Sylas.

He's fighting another one off from behind me, stabbing the spear into its chest. I twirl around, but trip back as a beast in front of me charges. I put my weight down on my knees, baring my balance, preparing my body for impact. Seconds later, our bodies collide and we both fly back from the force. I land on my side and it drops not too far away from me, right on the edge. Before it can recover, I jump to my feet, rush over to it and push it over the edge, watching it fall to the ground.

Sylas finishes off the beast he's fighting then tosses me the spear. I catch it effortlessly and we begin to run again, jumping acrobatically over gaps in the wall, stabbing abominations as they reach the top beside us. I pause for a moment, panting and sweating as I look back over the wall. The monsters seem endless. We've barely made a dent in their masses and they're starting to cover the top of the wall.

At the back of the crowd are the Highers, watching it all; watching what they've created, watching our numbers fade. To the side of them is Aiden, his dark eyes on me. Just to the side of him is the man that raised me, or so I thought.

Monarch.

Anger boils inside of me, making me feel like I could burst. The anger fuels my energy and I begin to move quicker, swinging the spear around and stabbing any beast near me, knocking one after the other to the ground. It feels like my spear is attached to my very arms, as though I'm not even holding onto it as I rip and tear into their flesh. They howl and nip at everything around them. I'm not even sure what's controlling me. Somehow, I've become the perfect soldier; however I'm doing this for good. Doing this to help mankind.

The herd of monsters begins to dwindle with my burst of energy and violence, but just as I think things are in our favor, I turn around, my jaw dropping. Dozens more are climbing the walls in waves, biting and clawing at the guards as they reach the top. Through my blind rage, I see something driving towards the wall with catastrophic force. An abomination, but it's different; stronger, bigger. It stands higher than everything else, at least twice as big as the rest with huge chunks of flesh hanging from its body, it's teeth razor sharp.

Before I can even react, it rams at top speed into the wall. There's a loud ripple and then the wall explodes like it was struck by dynamite. People are sent flying from the force. I'm thrown with them, unable to withstand the force.

Time slows down as people scream and fight around me.

Slow motion…

I can't think…

For a moment, I think I hear Sylas yelling at me in terror. Something's about to happen and then seconds later, I slam head first into the ground below.

Then everything goes dark.

Chapter 24

My eyes slowly open. Glimpses of people running and panicking flow through my mind. Some lie on the ground, motionless, some are screaming, others are groaning and working to get to their feet. Fires burn from torches and reflect into my eyes. I see the sky. It's dark. It hurts my head to look at it.

Footsteps surround me as the abominations begin to pour through the collapsed wall. Some of the guards and people start to run back into the city as they fight the hordes of monsters coming at them from all directions.

As I fade in and out of consciousness, I grasp the reality of the situation. We're going to be overrun. It's over. I think I always knew this would happen. Even when Maci was telling me I could do it. I refuse to give up, though. I must fight until the end.

But how can it all end if the monsters and Highers still exist?

Mustering up the last bit of strength I have, I snap myself out of my daze and try to get up. Pain shoots through my shoulder at the slightest bit of movement. It's out of place and I need to get it back in. I hold my breath and twist my body, grimacing as I feel a pop and it slides back into place. Warm liquid trickles from my head, yet I can already feel my body working to heal itself; mend my bones, bring the life back into me.

I glance around as I sit up straight, searching for a weapon. Just a ways in front of me, in a pile of broken metal and glass, is a dagger. I crawl over to it and pick it up. Then I breathe in and out, giving my body a few more minutes before I spring back to my feet and join the fight again.

The beasts are everywhere. On the wall, through the wall, running in through the gap in the wall. I quickly jump on top of one of the monsters that is ripping a person to pieces and stab it with my dagger, slicing its flesh apart. Blood spills out as it throws its head back and howls, however it lets go of the person in the process. I lift the dagger high above me as I hold onto its back then drive it down just below its head, sinking it in deep. It starts to run, but its knees give out and it falls to the ground, yelping.

I leap off its back with the dagger in my hand and charge at the herd of abominations barreling through the hole, ready to continue the battle even through the wall.

I spot Sylas jumping down from the wall, disappearing into the wave of their bodies. I want to cry out to him, but an abomination blindsides me and knocks me to the ground. I roll backwards and push myself upwards with my arms, launching into a flip. It nips at my ankles as I skitter to the side then slide the dagger through its enormous chest.

Another charges at me from the left. I spin around, steering the dagger downward, but it knocks it out of my hand. I grab ahold of its neck and pull it around with me as I glide to the ground, swoop up the dagger then swing us around. I stab it over and over again in its back. It lets out a roar, throwing its head back, hitting me in the chin before it falls to the ground as I stagger back from it, feeling my jaw pop out then back into place.

I pause to recover, but then something brushes my back. I instinctually spin around, my dagger ready to plunge it into the attacker, but I stop myself just in time as Sylas leans on me. He's covered in blood and looks exhausted, however I can see that there is still fight in him. He's not dying yet—we're not dying yet. Can we even die?

Blood trickles down his side and there's a large gash through his shirt and flesh.

"Are you okay?" I yell out as I glance around with the dagger out in front of me.

"Yeah, I'll be fine," he says, but I feel his lie all over him. "It's just a little scratch. I'll heal."

I swallow hard, feeling the end nearing. The wall is gone; cars are toppled on the ground in piles with bodies around me of both the abominations and people. Some of the people are rushing into their homes while others flee down the side of the wall, heading to the other end of the city. A few more are heading to the center of the city, trying to get away.

It hits me as the abominations chase them down towards the center of the city that we need to get somewhere where we can corner them. We need to keep them from heading further into the city towards the lab; somewhere where we can keep them from coming at us in all directions.

"Gather some of the Day Takers and follow me!" I yell to Sylas and to the people still alive around me. "We need to lead them another way!"

Sylas nods and then races off to gather them while I gather the stronger people around me. Once we all regroup, I take off and they follow me up the street.

"And make a lot of noise!" I shout out. When Sylas gives me a funny look, I add, "It'll get them to follow us and move them away from the weak."

He nods again and we make noise as we run down the street swiftly. I shout, trying to get the abominations to follow me, diverting them from going towards the lab. For the most part, it works. Many of them follow us, although some stay behind.

There are fires burning where people have fallen to the ground, dropping their torches, and blood stains the ground. Many of abominations are right on our heels, which is right where I want them. Finally, we reach the alley that Maci took me to earlier. I'm a little out of breath while, at the same time, my cuts aren't healing as quickly as they normally do.

"This is where we can hold them off without them attacking us from other sides," I say as we reach the alley with the people and even the Day Takers more out of breath then Sylas and I. "You four with spears line the width of the alley." I point at four people holding swords then move my finger to another group of people. "You two go herd more in our direction." I slide my finger to the Day

Takers. "And you stay behind me and wait for any to get through."

Everyone follows their orders, taking off in different directions. Seconds later, a handful of abominations rip around the corner, a herd of them at the others' heels. Their eyes bleed as they rush at us, their feet plowing at the ground. The front row target their spears and swords towards the front of the alley. Seconds later, the first group of abominations collides with their weapons. Sharp points pierce their rotting flesh and they die almost instantly, crumpling to the ground. More keep coming, though, and then the people behind me suddenly burst around in a panic and barrel towards the beasts.

"Stop!" I cry. "Fall back!"

They don't listen, and all I can do is fight. I stab the first abomination that reaches me and blood spurts all over my face. I tear the dagger from its body and spin into the next, stabbing at its chest. Sylas moves beside me, and we fight together, dipping and dodging as we slice through flesh, coating ourselves in their blood.

The abominations' bodies pile up at the alley and create a small barrier for us. My mood begins to lift as I think that maybe, just maybe, we can beat them. Then I hear a loud thudding noise that grows louder and louder before I then feel a ripple in the ground. I know before I see it what it is.

Moments later, the over-sized abomination charges around the corner of the building and down the alleyway at us. The rest of the abominations move out of the way, creating a path for it to get straight to the pile at the end of the alley and to us. There's nowhere to go and I'm not sure if we'll survive fighting it.

"What the hell do I do?" I mutter, glancing around at the Day Takers and people waiting for me to give them a command.

I feel someone touch my arm. I turn my head to meet Sylas's eyes.

"Run," he says in a low voice, his eyes pressing for me to listen.

I shake my head. "No... I'm not running away like a coward. What the hell are you talking about?"

His grip on my arm tightens as the massive beast starts to charge over the wall of abominations at the end of the alley. "You are the key to the cure. No one else," he presses. "Go back to the lab. Make sure that you get Mathew and the others out of here... make sure you survive."

He jerks me towards him and kisses me quickly. I barely register it before he's shoving me away, breathless. He whirls around, sprinting for the beast. Even though it tears me apart, I do what I have to do. I hurry and spring over the wall at the end of the alley, landing on the other side in another street, telling myself he'll make it. That he's a Day Walker. Deep down, I'm not sure, though. I'm not sure of anything anymore.

Blood stains the building walls and the ground below me. Horrifying screams blare at me from every angle, but I shut out the sight and run. I pass the blood and abominations, pass the bodies, pass all the death.

Was this all worth it? If Mathew's still alive, will he even be able to save everyone? Will I be able to go through with the fading?

I shove these thoughts from my mind when I reach the lab. Nichelle is gone, along with everyone else, except for one person lying dead on the ground. Her red hair is scattered across the blood stained ground, her flawless features frozen in time, like death managed to preserve her beauty. I feel my dead heart inside my chest ache for a second, taking in the death of Emmy.

She stares up at the sky, her eyes open, her arms lifelessly to her side. I crouch down and let my fingers drift over her eyelids, shutting her eyes, letting myself feel what I need to. Letting myself realize what I have to do.

I get to my feet and head for the door. There are signs of a struggle, blood splattered on the front section of the wall, boot tracks in the dirt leading away from the building, blood all around them.

I open the door and rush inside, running to the lab. It's quiet inside, however it looks untouched. The only signs of a mess are the vials everywhere, yet it was like that before.

"Mathew?" I call out quietly, vigilantly entering the room with my dagger out.

There's silence and then I hear a whimper as Mathew jumps up from behind the table. "Kayla." He glances over me; cuts and gashes, blood soaking my clothes. "God, what's going on out there?"

"Did you figure it out?" I ask, stepping towards him. "Please tell me you figured out if my blood and the virus replicates like it's supposed to."

"Not yet," he replies. "I'm still waiting to see if time will get the process moving." He glances down at his arms. "Like your blood did with me."

I walk to his side and rest my hand on his back, trying to shake out this bottomless, hopeless feeling. "You know you can fight, right?" I ask. "You don't have to hide behind tables."

He glances up at me. "I know, but I also don't want to risk the chance of dying, either. I need to figure all this out before I die. You and I… we need to make sure we survive so that we can move forward."

He waits expectantly for me to say that I'm with him, that I'll do the fading. My mouth opens, ready to give him my answer, but then I snap it shut when I hear the door open. I know it's not an abomination because they can't open doors, so I don't know who to expect.

When I turn my head and look in the direction of the doorway, I wish it'd been the abominations.

Gabrielle and Monarch are standing just inside the room with Aiden behind them. All three of their eyes are filled with the same coldness. The only difference between them is that Aiden is dressed in all black while Monarch and Gabrielle are in all white.

They're the same. God, poor Aiden.

"Bravo," Gabrielle says as he claps his hands together and enters the room. "You almost had us. Almost, but not quite. Yes, you put up a fight, but at the same time, there are still way more abominations over humans." He pauses, looking thoughtfully at Mathew. "Because Humans are weak."

I step in front of Mathew as he rises to his feet. "Run," I hiss at him. "Or prepare to fight."

Gabrielle snaps his fingers and in five lengthy strides, Aiden crosses the room. I move to hit him, but he catches my arm, matching, if not exceeding, my strength. He shoves me down to the ground and I crash against the table. As I scramble to my feet, he moves for Mathew, throwing his body into his.

They tumble into the cabinets, glass falling everywhere as they topple to the ground and roll around, throwing fists at each other. Mathew is still getting used to his power and he moves very sloppily compared to Aiden, causing them to move all over the floor and crash into things. Vials fall off the counters and shatter, pieces of glass surround them.

I start for them to pull Aiden off him, but Gabrielle grabs my arm, stopping me. I swing my other fist around and ram it into his jaw, but he's barely fazed by it as he pushes me effortlessly to the floor. I fall onto Mathew who's curled in a ball in front of Aiden's feet, giving up before this has even started.

Gabrielle chuckles as he slowly walks over to me, glass crunching under his feet. "I'll give it to you, Kayla, you're strong. You would have made a fine Higher if you weren't so determined to fight back, and go against rules and order. It's your one flaw, yet you're the cure to saving the Highers' breed." He shakes his head like he's so disappointed in this fact. "It's so pathetic that such an emotional girl is what's going to save the strongest and brightest species that's ever lived." He smiles as he glances down at himself, filled with vanity.

I search my mind, trying to figure out what to do next. Fight him? Run? What about Mathew? Will he run, too? Or will we fight? Do we even stand a chance? And what if I don't? What if the Highers capture me and are able to save their race? What would happen to the human race?

I'm not sure, but out corner of my eye I see the vial filled with black liquid that bubbles red. It's the easiest answer to all this. If it works, it gives the best outcome. Do I dare go through with it, though? Will it change me back to a human? Or will it change me into a shell of a human? Am I ready to give everything up? My life? My strength? My feelings for Sylas? My entire existence? Am I selfish or am I self-sacrificing?

"It doesn't matter what you do," Gabrielle continues as he paces the floor in front of me with his robe trailing behind him. "We're too strong, and in the end, you'll come with us and I'll find my cure."

You must save the world, Kayla, no matter what.

I feel the vial in my hand, the glass scorching hot against my skin. When I glance at Mathew to the side of me, he nods his head once, his eyes begging me to do it.

Gabrielle kicks me in the foot, bringing my attention back to him. "Get up and come now. It's time to give up and come back to the colony."

"Kayla, there are other things more important than Sylas and Aiden. Bigger things. There will come a time when you'll have to choose your battle, and may have to let someone go. You need to realize that you can't save every-

one. Not if you are going to save the world," Monarch presses, his eyes locked on me. "Do you understand?"

I understand. I wasn't created to fight against the Highers and vampires. I was created to end them. I bring my foot up and kick Gabrielle in the chin, putting as much force as I can muster behind it. As he buckles back, I jump to my feet and scurry over to the counter as Monarch and Aiden rush for me. I grab one of the syringes, bite off the cap from the needle and stab into the vial, filling the liquid. Then I drop the empty vial onto the floor and I hold out my wrist, pointing the needle to a vein in my arm.

I look Monarch straight in the eyes with no fear because if I feel the fear, then I won't go through with it. "I understand now," I say to him. "To save the world not everyone can survive."

I'm not sure if he understands me or not, but I don't care anymore. The needle plunges into my skin and the purple liquid enters my body. It burns in my veins like liquid fire. I drop like a ton of bricks to my knees, feeling sad, yet satisfied as I wait to fade.

"You stupid bitch!" Gabrielle screams as he races across the room at me. When he reaches me, he doesn't touch me; instead he picks up the vile beside me. He peers at it, trembling with rage. "What was that?"

I sit down on the ground as a euphoric state overcomes me, reclining against the counter, staring ahead at the wall. The burn in my veins stops and I feel oddly content and at peace as I feel this strange emptying sensation slithering through me. "It was the fading."

"Dammit! What have you done?" Gabrielle chucks the vile across the room, breaking it against the wall. Then he swipes his arm over the table, shattering vials and vials into pieces of glass, losing control of his emotions.

I look down at my arms expecting to see my skin fading, but everything looks normal. I'm not changing into anything, though, then again, will I even look different? What does fading even look like? Will I just vanish within myself and not even realize it?

Everyone watches me as I sit there, unmoving, unchanging... I don't feel different at all, just more content. Then I hear something that's not normal, like the tiny beat of a footstep; a small sound forming in my chest. I glance down at it, but see nothing. I can still hear it, though. *What's happening to me?*

Gabrielle starts to relax as he takes in the sight of my unchanging. "Well, look at you. All that bravery for nothing... even the fading can't work on you. You see, you're the perfect creation and soon you'll make the Highers the same way."

Ba-bump... ba-bump... ba-bump...

My heartbeat. Oh my God... I'm becoming a human. And it feels... invigorating because I can fully feel it, fully feel everything. My arms start to shake, tremble, weaken. My muscles deteriorate into the strength of a normal person. I feel my breath struggle a little more, my body stops healing, standing still; the wounds that were sealing themselves together pause and allow blood to trickle out.

Gabrielle's eyes burn with hatred as he sees it; his cure slipping away. He turns to Aiden with rage in his eyes, ready to throw all of it at someone. "Kill her... she's no use to me now."

I crawl back towards Mathew as he says it, feeling helpless. Shards of glass split at my skin. "No, Aiden, don't... please."

Aiden ignores me, nodding at Gabrielle and then marching towards me, his eyes cold and his expression hollow. I try to stand as Mathew gets to his feet, ready to protect me, but I fall back down, my legs weak and aching. I glance at Mathew for help, but Monarch rushes forward and pummels him, throwing his weight into him before both of them crash into the wall.

Aiden crouches down in front of me and cocks his head to the side, assessing me for a moment with his pale eyes that used to be honey brown and so beautiful. I miss those eyes.

"I'm sorry, Kayla," he says in a monotone voice. "I always have, and always will love you. Forever. Please forgive me." Then he opens his mouth, lets his fangs descend and then digs them into my vulnerable throat.

The sharp tips stab into my skin and straight into my muscles. I feel myself about to split apart, wanting to cry out or beg as hopelessness crushes me down.

Moments later, I feel myself drifting away and can feel the cure for mankind drifting away with me. I struggle to hold on, but the room fades around me as I sink to the ground. Aiden covers himself over me, drinking from my veins. The more gulps he gets, the weaker I become, and I know that soon I'll be gone. Dead.

And the cure might die with me.

Suddenly, Aiden jerks back, letting out a growl. My eyes widen as I sit up, bleeding out all over myself, watching in horror as Aiden clutches his head and falls to the floor. He screams so loudly it rings in my ears. His body begins to flail as every one of his muscles spasms.

Gabrielle's expression collapses as he grips onto the table, watching Aiden roll around on the ground, shouting out and begging for help. "What did you do to him?"

I shake my head and press my hand to my bleeding neck as I crawl across the floor, feeling somewhat normal again while Aiden continues to go into a crazy fit of frenzy.

I wonder what's happening to him. If he's hurt. If he'll die. Although Aiden did terrible things, I know it wasn't by his own choice. He's connected to the Highers, broken by Monarch. He's still my friend and I don't want to see him die.

I don't know how to help him, though, and my arms are giving out as I lose more and more blood while it also feels like I'm losing something else. My arm gives out on me and I fall flat onto my stomach, listening to my heart beat as glass pokes at my skin from beneath me. Something feels different about me. I almost feel... human. Not just physically, but... well, emotionally. I don't know how to process this; all the stuff flooding my body at once. Pain. Ache. Hurt. Sadness for Aiden and what he's going through. Love. Not for Aiden, but maybe for another. Sylas. I don't know if he's still alive and it stings.

It starts to grow quiet as I sift through my emotions and then realize Aiden has stilled. When I push myself up enough to look around, I see that Gabrielle and Monarch are standing over him as he lies lifelessly on the ground.

"Is he dead?" Gabrielle asks Monarch.

"Does it really matter?" Monarch replies.

Gabrielle shrugs then shakes his head and starts to turn away when suddenly Aiden's eyes pop open. I catch my breath, feeling... happy as I take in the honey brown color of his eyes. The way he was before. He's cured. I can tell by the emotion flooding in his eyes. It's evidence of the old Aiden... the one that cared about the world, humanity; that cared about everything.

He turns his head and scans the room. "What happened?" he asks in a stupor, gripping his head. His hair has glass in it and his skin has cuts, yet he seems so much happier than before. "Where am I, Kayla?"

"You're back," I say, choking on my happiness, but then I gasp as Gabrielle's pale eyes slide to me. They almost look red.

His fangs slip out from his veins as he snarls. "I've had enough of this!" he cries, enraged. Underneath the anger, I see a hint of fear when he looks at me. He no longer can see his cure to perfection.

I try to scurry to my feet as he races towards me, fueled by his anger, shoving the table out of the way. My human legs feel rubbery and unnatural, and I can barely get my knees to bend as I lose more blood from my neck. I start to shut my eyes and hold my breath when I see Aiden get to his feet and run for me.

"No!" I cry as he collides with Gabrielle's body and they both tumble to the ground. I force my legs to move and manage to stumble unsteadily to my feet. I stagger towards them, moving slower than I ever thought was possible. It doesn't matter how fast I move, though. I'm too late.

Gabrielle already has Aiden pinned under him with his fangs deep in his throat. My knees knock together as I stumble over to them, grabbing ahold of Gabrielle's robe, trying to pull him off Aiden, but I'm jerked back and tossed aside by Monarch.

My head slams against the hard ground. The room spins as I sit up, clutching my bleeding neck. I feel like I'm dying inside as I watch Gabrielle and Monarch feed off Aiden, devouring his blood and tearing at his flesh. I remember how Mathew said they'd once drank human blood. The taste of Aiden's seems to be driving them to want more.

My heart starts to ache as wet droplets slip from my eyes and burn at my skin while I crawl towards them, wanting to help, although I'm helpless. I feel hatred. Anger. Rage. The need to get revenge. I feel out of control. Feel the desire for my strength back.

I hate this.

I hate being human.

Blood soaks their white robes, and when they finally stop feeding, they turn their heads to look at me. Their faces, lips and hair are dripping with Aiden's blood as an uncontrolled look encompasses their eyes. My initial reaction is to rush forward and claw their eyes out, but I'm not strong enough for that. So, even though I don't want to, I back away.

They follow my movement, coming at me with their backs hunched over, looking more and more like the vampire breed. I pick up a piece of glass and throw it at them, but it barely flies two feet.

Mathew starts to step forward to help me when Monarch lunges at him and lets out a cry. Gabrielle smiles at me then he zips forward, jumping at me. He ends up tripping over his feet, however, and lets out a wail as he falls on his face. I'm not sure I've ever seen a Higher make a mistake like that. When he starts to vibrate and spasm, I suddenly understand why.

Gabrielle struggles to control his body, flapping his arms around and pushing his feet against the floor. He screams and shouts and flails just like Aiden did, fear filling his reddened eyes. I watch, feeling this sick satisfaction rise within me, as though him suffering somehow makes up for Aiden, when it doesn't. Aiden is gone and nothing will bring him back.

I'm about to start crying again when I hear commotion at my right. I glance over and Monarch is doing the exact same thing as Gabrielle, both of them at a loss of control of their bodies. Mathew watches with me as we observe them slipping away towards humanity. Their bodies slam into tables, knocking things over, spilling the contents around the room. Vials break, shatter, pooling the floor with liquid.

Then, just as quickly as it began, it stops. Silence takes over as they still; their skin cut up by the glass while their white robes remain stained with blood. Their eyes are the dead giveaway of what's happened, though. Monarch's are no longer pale, they're dark grey like the sky, and Gabrielle's are an alarming shade of green.

They're human again. Life and breath and blood stream through their veins.

Gabrielle rolls over to his stomach, moaning as he battles to stand to his feet. He gives up at sitting and then scoots across the floor to the upturned silver table. He peers in the reflective surface, examining his reflection closely. "This is impossible!" he yells, looking over at Monarch who is still lying on the ground, staring at his arms, his hands shaking. "How could this cure us? Why!"

Mathew and I exchange a look and then Mathew gives me a small smile. My blood not only still holds the cure, but it replicates like the virus he injected into me earlier. It worked. The risks we took worked, and now we can save the human race.

Monarch turns over onto his stomach and uses his arms to push himself up to sit. It takes him a moment to get there and then I can see a new look in his eyes; one I've never seen before. Happiness. "Because she's perfection," he answers Gabrielle.

Gabrielle goes into a fury and begins to throw everything within his reach—vials, flask, syringes—yet all that ends up doing is making his arm tired. He kicks his foot at the nearest chair and swears profusely, cursing me and what I've done to him.

What *I've* done to him. This sentence hits me harder than anything that I have ever felt before. It's over, yet it seems as if it's only starting. The cure is inside me and in Gabrielle and Monarch and Mathew, but there's still so much more to do.

"We have a cure," I whisper in awe, glancing down at my bloody arms. My blood.

"You did this to me," Gabrielle says as he staggers closer to me, barely able to stand. "You did this." He gasps for air. So weak. "You've undone all that we have worked for. Everything I've done..." He lands on top of me as his hands go around my neck and I gasp. He presses his weight down on me, his face reddening as he shoves me down against the floor. "I'll kill you!" he growls. I can see in his eyes that he will.

I feel my breath leaving me as I try to fight—try to kick, try to get away—but I don't know how to work my body. The feeling of the helplessness is frightening. Death. Weakness. Is that what being human is?

I shut my eyes as I push on Gabrielle's chest, refusing to give up; using all the strength I have in me. I feel him leave my body and I think that maybe, just maybe, I've somehow gotten over my human weakness. When I open my eyes, though, I find that Monarch and Mathew have pulled Gabrielle off me and Monarch's shoving him down to the floor.

"Go," he says to Mathew and me as Gabrielle fights to get away. Monarch picks up a piece of glass as he says, "Go check on your people."

Mathew hurries across the room, but I don't dare move as Monarch presses the tip of the glass to Gabrielle's throat. "You and I have some unfinished business."

"Monarch, don't," I say, feeling something ache deep inside my chest, knowing if he kills him, he might feel the same ache. "It's not... it's not worth more blood on your hands."

Monarch turns around and looks at me, his grey still a bit alarming. "Kayla, go. You've done your part, and now I'll do mine."

I don't want to leave and let Monarch do what I think he's going to do—kill Gabrielle—yet at the same time, I see nothing except evil in Gabrielle's eyes. So even though it's agonizing, I turn and walk away, hating myself a little bit.

When I step outside, it's still dark; however, I can see a speck of sun on the horizon and I swear I can feel it's warmth. The streets are fairly quiet, the echoes of battle continuing in the distances. The streets are covered with bodies of abominations and people. For the most part, though, the people and Day Takers—what's left of them— have gotten the streets under control from the beasts.

Near the corner of the building, Nichelle is hugging Mathew, sobbing as torches burn in the street. "You're okay." Tears stream down her face as she grips him tightly.

I can suddenly understand her emotion more than I'd like to admit.

He holds her firmly in return. "It was all Kayla," he says. "We owe it all to her, for risking her life to save others."

I stop when he says it and glance around at the blood painted on the streets. Yes, there's a cure now, but at what cost? All these deaths... and Aiden's death... and there's still so much left to change. How are we even going to get it to spread quickly enough? How are we going to fight to cure the world? Yet, as I glance around again at the streets, hope arises because we survived.

I'm about to take off and see if I can find Sylas when Nichelle rushes over to me and hugs me, tears spilling from her eyes while I have to choke back my own. I wrap one arm around her as she thanks me repeatedly. It doesn't feel as strange as it used to. When I let her go, she runs back to Mathew and continues to hug him. They seem completely happy and so do I, yet the death that surrounds us also makes me incredibly sad.

"Are you okay?" The voice takes me by surprise and I spin around, almost falling to the ground as my weak human legs try to give up on me.

Sylas catches me in his arms and pulls me against his chest, holding my weight for me. The warmth of his touch overflows me, along with my feelings for him, and what I have to tell him. Tears start to fall from my eyes again, despite how much I attempt to suck them back.

"I'm so sorry," I say as I circle my arms around him.

"Sorry for what?" he asks, kissing my hair.

"Aiden," I choke.

He tenses and holds me tighter. I know he won't cry. Not when he's still a Day Walker, but deep beneath the surface, he'll hurt. I hate being the one to tell him the thing that will make him feel that way.

"Kayla... why do you smell different?" he asks, his face nestled against my neck.

"Because I'm human," I whisper.

He jerks away and looks me in the eyes, searching them, and then his expression falls. I wonder if he hates me. If he'll leave me here, standing in the streets, alone.

"What happened?" he asks, shocked.

"I took the fading." I take a deep breath then blow it out and it feels like I'm blowing out freedom. "And now we found a cure."

Epilogue

It all seems too good to be true, and for the next few days, we're all stuck in some strange, alternate reality, but for once our hopes are high because we have a future of our own.

The people of the colony spend a lot of time burying their loved ones and cleaning up their city. There were a lot of deaths, including humans and Day Takers. Maci and Greyson managed to make it out okay, along with Mathew and Monarch, who are making plans for the best way to spread the cure without killing off the entire population of the world. They decide the best way is to send the remaining Day Takers out there to inject the vampires with my blood and allow them to spread the cure amongst them. I'm a little wary of his plan since it follows his whole army theory he's had from the start. Still, it seems like the best plan for going up against the vampires and the remaining Highers. Plus, it's the only plan we have now, however Mathew and Monarch are trying to make the cure airborne.

There's one more reason why I'm not so keen on the idea of the Day Takers being the ones who have to go. But that's based on the fact that the person I care for the most is a Day Taker turned Day Walker. One who's been pretending not to be sad, yet I can see it in his eyes whenever he doesn't think I'm looking at him, and the fact that he doesn't seem to want to bury his brother, not wanting to accept yet.

However, on the third day of recovery, Sylas and I decide to have a burial after he finally decides it's time to move on. Around daybreak, we go up to the top of the highest hill and Sylas digs a large hole. Then we put Aiden's body into it and bury it with sand. By the time we're finished, the sunlight is breaking through the sky and, for some reason, it looks brighter.

"Are you ready to go back to the town?" I ask Sylas as he stares out at the land, wisps of his dark hair shadowing his charcoal eyes.

He shakes his head and sits down in the dirt. "Not yet." He glances up at me then pats the ground beside him. I do what he asks and sit down beside him.

When I get situated, he reaches over and takes my hand. I can immediately sense that something's wrong, but I'm afraid to ask what because, knowing Sylas, he'll give me the blunt truth whether I like it or not.

"I've been wanting to talk to you about some stuff," he starts, leaning back on his arms and watching the horizon, watching the sun rise. "You have the cure inside you, and everyone's talking about spreading it across the world... changing everyone back to being human and how the Day Takers are going to be the main ones to do it."

"It's not a bad thing." I keep my eyes on the approaching sunlight. "Although I wish you weren't going."

"Do you mean that?" he asks, stretching his legs.

I nod. "Of course I do." I cup his cheek and force him to look at me, the daylight reflecting in his eyes. The perfect creation right before me, which makes me feel small, but at the same time, protected. "I know you don't want to hear it, but I don't want you to go out there and fight. I want you to stay here with me."

He looks away from me, out at the desert land again. It's so quiet, mainly because many of the vampires around here have been cured already. This town has sort of turned into a sanctuary.

"Good," he finally says quietly without looking at me. "Because I want to be cured by you. Right now."

"Wait? You're not going to put a fight up about this?" I sort of thought he would if I ever got the courage to ask him. I thought he'd tell me no because, honestly, if I had a choice in the matter, I probably would have.

He shakes his head and then looks at me, his eyes as black as singed wood. "I was going to, but then I started thinking... about you... and how much happier you look right now." He touches his finger to the side of my eyes. "How beautiful these look even though you're scared." He traces a line from my eyes to my lips. "And how I just want us to live a normal life together, like we would have done if the world hadn't changed." He pauses as he thinks back, smiling to himself. "I just want to be with you."

I swallow hard at his emotional words. I've actually been really emotional since I turned human and I both love it and hate it, but I'm hoping that once I get used to it, it'll be easier.

I nervously hold my arm out. "Then be with me."

He smiles softly, his eyes darkening as he takes my arm in his hand. "Are you sure that's what you want?" he asks, arching his brow. "For me to be with you."

I hesitate and then nod, telling the truth and arrogance rises on his face. It doesn't piss me off though and I'm starting to accept that Sylas's cockiness is something that pulls me to him.

Abruptly his fangs slip out, making me jump. His smile broadens at my tension and then he starts to lower his mouth to my arm, keeping his dark eyes on me the entire time. He places a delicate kiss on my forearm, breathing in my scent one last time before the tips of his teeth graze my skin. He pauses, taking a ravenous inhale, and then plunges his fangs deep into my skin.

Lightheadedness overpowers me as he savors my blood, his neck muscles tightening as he drinks. His eyes flutter shut and, for a second, I wonder if he'll drink all of me, if he'll lose control.

Moments later, however, his teeth leave my arm and then he falls to the ground, screaming and twisting, his face contorted in pain. It hurts too much to watch and I have to look away at the sunlight to try to block it out, balling my hands into fists. I hold my breath until it grows quiet—until I know for sure that his pain has stopped—then I look back at him.

He's lying motionless beside me in the sand, his arms and legs limp with my blood staining his lips.

I kneel beside him and examine him over. "Sylas, can you hear me?"

His eyelids gradually lift open to show eyes that are no longer black, they're bright blue. The sunlight reflects in them, making them look beautiful.

"Did it work?" he asks dazedly.

I nod, smiling, overwhelmed with relief and happiness as I lean down and press my lips to his. We kiss until the sun is fully up then we finally break apart and sit side by side, holding hands, watching the land, feeling the wind and breathing in the air as both of our hearts beat freely.

The land looks different, more alive, cacti growing in the sand, lizards and snakes scurrying back and forth. Even the sky looks clearer, the sun brighter and warmer. Maybe it's just me looking at things differently. Because for once I have hope. A hope for tomorrow. A hope for humanity.

A hope for a future.

Jessica Sorensen

The New York Times and USA Today bestselling author, Jessica Sorensen, lives in the snowy mountains of Wyoming. When she's not writing, she spends her time reading and hanging out with her family.

Other books by Jessica Sorensen:

The Coincidence of Callie and Kayden (The Coincidence, #1)

The Secret of Ella and Micha (The Secret, #1)

Shattered Promise (Shattered

The Fallen Star (Fallen Star Series, Book 1)

The Underworld (Fallen Star Series, Book 2)

The Vision (Fallen Star Series, Book 3)

The Promise (Fallen Star Series, Book 4)

The Lost Soul (Fallen Souls Series, Book 1)

Darkness Falls (Darkness Falls Series, Book 1)

Darkness Breaks (Darkness Falls Series, Book 2)

Ember (Death Collectors, Book 1)

Connect with me online:

http://jessicasorensen.com

http://www.facebook.com/#!/JessicaSorensensAd
ultContemporaryNovels?notif_t=page_new_likes

http://www.facebook.com/pages/Jessica-
Sorensen/165335743524509

https://twitter.com/#!/jessFallenStar

Darkness Fades

Printed in Great Britain
by Amazon